MYSTIC PORTAL

MYSTIC PORTAL

Another 'You Say Which Way' Adventure
by
Eileen Mueller

For mountain-bikers and adventurers, everywhere.

Published by:
The Fairytale Factory Ltd.
Wellington, New Zealand.
All rights reserved.
Copyright Eileen Mueller © 2016

YouSayWhichWay.com

ISBN-13: 978-1537629674
ISBN-10: 1537629670

How this book works

- This story depends on YOU.

- YOU say which way the story goes.

- What will YOU do?

At the end of each chapter, you get to make a decision. Turn to the page that matches your choice. **P62** means turn to page 62.

There are many paths to try. You can read them all over time. Right now, it's time to start the story. Good luck.

Oh … and watch out for Bog, the ogre!

Mystic Portal

Enter Mystic Portal

Standing on a grassy knoll high above the sea, you pull on your biking gloves. Next to you, Sidney checks his full-face helmet. Your breath is a misty cloud in the crisp morning air. Tracey zips her jacket shut over her body armor – she's got all the latest mountain biking gear.

Fastening her racing goggles, and tightening her helmet, Tracey calls, "My lid's good. Ready when you are."

Sidney glances at the trail leading down into the trees and bites his lip. Aside from your helmets and gloves, you and Sidney only have shin guards.

He's not the only one who's nervous. Breakfast is dancing in your stomach as if it knows you're about to enter Mystic Portal. The entrance to the track is a dark gaping hole in the pine forest. Toadstools stand guard on either side of a thin dirt trail heading downwards through the trees. At the bottom of the track is a sandy beach. Expert riders usually make it to the beach by lunchtime. It's not the entrance or the beach you're worried about, just all the tough obstacles in between.

You've all been training for months for this downhill ride. The three of you met at Tracey's house yesterday to tune your bikes. You all adjusted your shocks, bled your brakes, lubricated your chains and pumped your tires.

"I can hardly believe we're finally doing this," Tracey murmurs with a smile. "I'm glad we've already walked the trail a few times, so we know it."

"Me too." Sidney is nibbling his lip again.

Nudging him, you ask, "Still want to go?" Hopefully he'll back out, so you can keep him company.

Tracey rolls her eyes. "Not so fast, guys. You're not chicken, are you? We planned this. You can't go home now."

She's onto you. Just your luck.

Sidney's eyes flick back to the track. "Jase said weird things happen when you go down Mystic Portal."

"But it was fine when we walked it," says Tracey.

"Things that don't happen when you walk down," says Sidney, "only when you bike. You guys sure you want to go?"

"Jase says new jumps appear overnight." You fight to keep your voice steady.

"Yeah," says Sidney, "and other jumps vanish."

Tracey smiles at Sidney. "Okay, I'm nervous too, but if you want to take my bike, I'll go on your hard-tail."

Tracey has a top-of-the-range mountain bike, a

downhill racing dualie, with the latest greatest shock absorbers on the front and rear suspension.

Sidney's hard-tail is a cheap mountain bike with no back suspension, so he hits the ground hard when he lands. Yours is a dirt jump bike without gears – even simpler than Sidney's. You've both had a turn on Tracey's new bike. It feels like you're landing on a giant marshmallow.

But neither of you can afford a bike like hers.

Sidney's eyes linger on Tracey's bike as he considers her offer. "Nah, I'm fine," he says, toughing it out.

"We can always use the chicken lines," you say. "We don't have to do every jump."

"Let's go," says Sidney, jutting out his jaw. He doesn't want to be the one to chicken out.

You know how he feels.

You get on your bikes.

Tracey zooms down the track, chewing up the dirt with her tires. Sidney's close behind, crunching over broken twigs and pine needles. Hard on his tail, you go over a tiny rise in the track and pull your handlebars upwards, lifting your bike off the ground.

"Hey you guys, I got some air." You yell, landing with a smack.

Sidney whoops.

"First jump is Camel Hump," Tracey yells as she goes past a makeshift sign with a badly painted camel on it.

Who built these cool jumps?" asks Sidney.

"No idea," she calls. "They say it's a mystery."

Tracy takes a corner tightly, stomping her foot on the ground. Sidney sticks to the middle of the trail, nice and safe, cruising around the corner. You rush at the corner, going high on the berm, then speed down the bank, back onto the track.

Ahead, the track splits in two.

"I'm taking Camel Hump," calls Tracey. "You coming or are you going to play chicken, Sidney?"

"I want to get to Ogre Jaws. The faster the better," calls Sidney. "That's the coolest jump ever."

You have to agree with him. Ogre Jaws is a great jump — it even has teeth. You can't wait to try it.

He crows like a rooster, then veers off to the left, bypassing the jump and going down the easier trail. He disappears into the trees, clucking like a chicken.

Tracey swoops up the steep reddish rise of Camel Hump. "Coming?" she calls. Her bike flies into the air, then disappears.

No, that can't be right. She can't have disappeared. She must've landed beyond your line of sight. Either that, or you've gone crazy.

Your spine prickles. Or has she really vanished? Weird things happen on this track.

You're nearing the fork in the trail. To your right is Camel Hump. To your left is the way out — the chicken line, which leads to Dino Drop and Ogre Jaws.

It's time to make a decision. Do you:

Hit Camel Hump? **P6**

Or

Bypass Camel Hump and go down the chicken line?
P46

Hit Camel Hump

Your tires hum up the red compacted dirt of Camel Hump and hit the jump. The trees blur. Your bike is airborne. For a glorious moment you're flying – this is what you love.

The forest and Mystic Portal disappear.

You land with a whump. Your suspension is terrible, and you're swaying from side to side. Wait, this isn't your bike. What is it?

Rubbing your eyes, you squint against bright light and focus. You're on an animal, a camel, plodding down an enormous red sand dune. That's why you're swaying. You pitch forward, grabbing a handle on the camel's saddle to save yourself from doing an endo – wait would it still be called an endo if you go over the top of camel's head instead of over handlebars?

Another dune looms in front of you. The only things you can see are the deep-blue sky and endless red sand.

Where's Mystic Portal?

And where is Tracey? She went over Camel Hump before you and vanished in midair. She must be here somewhere.

"Tracey!" you yell. "Tracey, where are you?"

No answer. Only scorching heat beating down. A bead of sweat stings your eye. The air shimmers with heat waves. Dry air parches your throat. You're already thirsty and you've only just got here – wherever here is.

The camel plods on, making its way down the sand with even steps. It's a weird sensation, feeling as if you're going to tumble off the camel as it heads downwards. You soon find that leaning back helps you stay balanced in the saddle. At least there are cushions to pad your butt – you'd imagined camel humps to be soft, but there's nothing soft about the hump you're sitting on.

You pat the creature's back. "Hey, boy, thanks for giving me a ride. It sure beats walking in this sand."

The camel doesn't answer, but it does snort. You smile. Maybe it's not answering because it's a girl and you got it wrong. You laugh – the heat's affecting you already. Everyone knows camels don't understand people.

Soon the camel reaches the bottom of the dune, traipses across the sand and starts climbing the next dune. Maybe there'll be something interesting over the top. There has to be more to this place than dunes.

You were wrong. When you reach the top of the next rise, for miles in every direction, all you see is red.

You breathe through your nose, hoping it will cool the air so your throat isn't quite so parched, but it's so hot your nostrils feel like they're on fire.

"Not fair," you mumble. "How am I ever going to get out of here? I thought I was going for a bike ride."

It's then you notice the camel's leather harness is the same green and red as your bike. Astounded, you glance down at the saddle. It's red with silver edging, and so are the cushions – like your bike seat! Has your bike somehow transformed into a camel? Is that what Jase meant by strange things happening when you ride Mystic Portal? What on earth?

Or are you on earth at all?

With a sinking feeling, you realize it's no coincidence that jumping over Camel Hump has landed you on camelback.

A shriek sounds behind you. You whirl, grabbing hold of a brown bundle behind the saddle to save yourself from falling. Making its way toward you is a weird bird.

More than weird. Bizarre. Its wings are trailing stray feathers. Its body is way larger than a normal bird, and it flaps strangely. Usually birds flap evenly, but this thing moves haphazardly. Dangerously.

A giant desert vulture? Looking for a snack? You lean forward and pat the camel. "Come on, let's get going." As if the camel understands you, it plunges down the next dune. Soon you're hidden.

But not for long. The thing's shrieks grow closer. Something swoops overhead. Your hair ruffles. Oh, no, you're no longer wearing your bike helmet.

The bird shrieks again and swoops toward your head, narrowly missing you. "Hey," it cries, in a familiar voice, "why are you ignoring me?"

"Tracey?"

She swoops in front of you, hovering in the air beside the camel's head. It's not a bird after all! Tracey's on a tattered threadbare mat. A green and gold mat – the same colors as her bike.

"Steady," she snaps.

The flying carpet bucks and sways, nearly tipping her off.

You stifle a laugh. She had such a new shiny bike and now she's on the rattiest tattiest carpet you've ever seen. Your camel beats that old rag any day.

"What's so funny?" Tracey glowers as the carpet swerves, loose threads trailing behind it. She shoves her fist through a hole and grabs on to the edge with white knuckles. "I said *steady!*"

The carpet ignores her. Why wouldn't it? It's only a carpet – even if it is a flying one.

"Climb aboard and help me," she calls.

There's no way you're getting on that thing. It's way too dangerous. At least your camel is stable. As you shake your head, the carpet tries to buck her off again.

You can't help laughing out loud. "That thing's like a bucking bronco."

"Nah, more like a rollercoaster. You too chicken to ride it?"

"No way, I'm not chicken!"

"Yeah, I know you're braver than that." She raises an eyebrow. "You gonna help me?"

"Of course. I'll get on board!"

A deep voice comes out of nowhere, "You don't have to go with that tatty old thing. I'm a desert survival specialist and I can transport you to an oasis."

"What?" You gaze around. "Who was that?" You, Tracey, the carpet and the camel are the only things you can see – apart from sky and endless sand.

"It's me, Jamina. Didn't you know camels talk?"

Wow, your camel understands you. Amazing. It may even be better than a bike!

"Come on," says Tracey. "I can't really fly this thing, but you'll probably be excellent. I need your help."

Travelling by flying carpet would be exciting.

Jamina turns her head around, snuffling at your hand. "Don't you want to see the oasis and meet all the people who live there?"

Being with a talking camel sounds exciting too.

It's time to make a decision. Do you:

Stay with Jamina the talking camel? **P11**

Or

Go with Tracey on the tatty flying carpet? **P24**

Stay with Jamina the talking camel

Tracey's carpet does a wild swerve and she slips, grabbing a fistful of tassels, her legs dangling off the side of the carpet. "Please," she says, "I really need your help."

"Sorry, Tracey," you say, "that thing looks too dangerous for me. Besides, Jamina is going to take me to an oasis. I'm looking forward to that."

"Don't blame you," she says. "Wish I had a camel." The carpet bucks, dumping Tracey onto its middle. Sprawled on the carpet, one of her feet hangs through a hole. "Hey, you." She punches the carpet. "What do you think you're doing? *Steady*, I said. *Steady*."

But the carpet seems to have a mind of its own. Zipping and bucking, it takes off across the desert – with Tracey yelling at it.

"Some tourists never learn," says Jamina. "The secret to training a flying carpet is speaking politely. Your friend is going to have a tough time."

"Why didn't you tell her?" you ask.

"People learn better when they figure things out themselves," says Jamina. "Are you thirsty?"

"Absolutely parched."

"Do you have any water with you?"

Of course. In your backpack. Feeling foolish, you reach for your forgotten water bottle to have a long drink.

Jamina interrupts you. "Not too much," she says. "It's better to take small sips often than to run out and go for hours without water."

You're so thirsty you could drink the whole thing in one go, but Jamina is the desert survival specialist so, after a few gulps, you stow your water bottle in your backpack. "I don't know much about camels, but I'm keen to learn. I thought all camels had two humps, but you only have one."

Jamina snorts loudly, fine-grained sand flying from her nostrils. "Asian camels have two humps. Camels in Arabia, like me, have one. We're called dromedaries."

"So you're a dromedary?"

"I am," she replies. "How do you like the desert so far?"

You squint at the bright glare on the horizon and the miles of sand around you. "It's… um… hot."

Jamina stops, her large even feet creating depressions in the sand, and turns her head to gaze at you. "You're not wearing a hat. You could get sunstroke."

"I don't have a hat with me," you say. Fishing around in your backpack, you pull out a light sweatshirt and tie it over your head.

"That's better," Jamina says. "The first rule of desert survival is to drink water slowly, the second is to shade your head so your body doesn't have to work so hard to keep cool."

A refreshing breeze wafts across the sand, creating beautiful ripples on the surface. Jamina sniffs the air and continues walking, but faster. At first the wind feels good, cooling your skin, but soon it whips sand into your eyes, making them sting.

Jamina picks up speed, running down another dune, then stops. "A sand storm is coming. We'd better take shelter," she says.

There's nowhere to shelter. Nothing but sand. What is she talking about? She bends her front knees to kneel, nearly tipping you over her head, then bends her rear knees too. She's sitting down in the sand.

Panic grips you. Shouldn't she be running to get away from the storm? She said to take shelter, but how? You could hunker down next to her, hiding your face in her furry side. Or you could convince her to outrun the storm.

"Jamina, how fast can dromedaries run?"

"Forty miles per hour, but only in short bursts."

Really fast. Surely she could outrun that pesky wind. "Shouldn't we run?" you ask.

"We could try," she says. "Or we could pitch our tent and take shelter inside."

Our tent? You glance behind the saddle at the brown bundle you grabbed earlier to stop you from falling off. It's a tent.

The wind is getting stronger, flinging hard grains of

sand at you, stinging your arms with fierce nips.

You don't have long to make a decision. Do you:

Pitch the tent to take shelter from the sand storm? **P15**

Or

Encourage Jamina to run from the sandstorm? **P23**

Pitch the tent to take shelter from the sand storm

Wind whistles between the dunes. A fine mist of sand swirls in the air, coating your teeth with grit. Climbing off her saddle, you untie the tent from Jamina's back and shake it out.

The tent's shaped like an igloo with a zipper in the door, an inner layer of mesh, and a floor sealed to the sides. You snap two long poles together and thread them through the fabric so the crossed poles curve over the roof and sides. You drive the unusually-long tent pegs deep into the sand.

Over the dunes, in the distance, a great red cloud of sand billows into the sky. The storm is approaching swiftly. You dive into the tent and pull the zipper shut.

Within moments, sand strikes your tent, pattering against the light fabric.

A voice asks, "Can you unzip the door a little so I can put my nose in? The sand is stinging my eyes."

It's Jamina. She's carried you all this way, now she's stuck out in the storm. You unzip the tent a fraction and she shoves her head inside at floor level. Pulling the zip down tight against her neck, you make sure the fabric is secure so no sand can sneak in.

Hundreds of tiny dark spots beat against the tent. Wind whistles around you, shaking the fabric. Soon the drumming of the sand is a dull roar.

"Jamina, why do you have your nostrils shut? I didn't know camels could do that."

"Keeps the sand out." She snorts, flaring her nostrils again. "Maybe it's time for some desert stories. I know a few. Would you like one?"

It looks like you're going to be stuck here a while. Opening your backpack, you pull out a sandwich. "A story sounds great. Would you like a bite?"

Jamina snorts at your sandwich. "No thanks. My hump is a great storage cupboard, allowing me to go for days without food or water. Unless it's good food." Her eyes slide along your sandwich and her nose wrinkles, as if it's a rotting rat.

Her voice croons as she starts the story. "Once upon a time, there was a Bedouin with his camel, Jim, out in the desert when a sand storm struck. The Bedouin was clever–"

"Hang on," you say. "Why does the camel have a name, but the Bedouin doesn't?"

Jamina snorts. "Everyone knows that camels are the main character in desert jokes, not humans. Besides, Jim was my grandfather." She snorts again.

Her snorting's beginning to become a habit. Do all camels snort this much? "Oh, all right," you concede. "The Bedouin doesn't have to have a name then."

"The Bedouin was clever. He had a tent with him so, when the sand storm hit, he quickly pitched it and climbed inside. The storm was ferocious, making his tent buck. Soon Jim was braying outside. "Please let me put my nose just inside the door,' he cried. 'The sand is stinging my eyes terribly.' "

"Hey that's what you did!"

Jamina's lips pull back, showing her teeth — a comical-looking camel smile.

You grin back. "So, what happened?"

"The Bedouin let Jim the camel put his head inside the tent. The wind grew fiercer, whipping great gusts of sand at the tent, like a giant playing in a sand pit. 'Ow! The sand is stinging my shoulders,' Jim whimpered. 'Could I just put my shoulders in the tent to protect them?' What do you think the Bedouin did?"

"He let Jim bring his shoulders in," you reply.

"Do you know this story?" asks Jamina.

"No, I've never heard it before. I'm just good at guessing."

"Once Jim had his shoulders inside, the roar of the sandstorm grew even louder. 'Oh, my flanks ache. I'm sure my hide is raw. Could I please bring my hindquarters inside?' What do you think the Bedouin did?"

"Let Jim in?"

"Of course he did. He was a kind man, but a foolish one."

"Why was he foolish?"

"Just wait and see." Jamina snorts again.

"Jim heaved his back end inside, and the Bedouin zipped the tent shut, leaving only Jim's tail outside. Soon Jim was moaning again. 'My tail, my poor tail is being flayed to pieces by the vicious sand. What–"

"– do you think the Bedouin said," you finish the sentence for her. This story is getting rather predictable. "Of course the Bedouin let Jim bring his tail in." You're sure you're giving Jamina the right answer because she gives you one of her funny camel smiles again.

"That's right," says Jamina. "But by now there was no room for the foolish Bedouin, so Jim kicked him out into the sandstorm." She starts to bray. A weird guttural chuckling sound fills the tent.

She sounds so funny, you can't help laughing too, but a strange prickle travels down your spine. Is she warning you? Is she about to toss you out in the sand storm to die?

"Is this a joke?" you ask.

"No," she says, between chuckles.

"I hope your shoulders are alright," you say. "You don't need to bring them inside the tent, do you?" There's no way you'll let her, even if she asks.

Her chuckling bray grows louder.

You're about to block your ears when she stops.

"Of course not," she says. "I'm civilized and come from a long line of respected camels. I'd never do that to my riders."

"Respected camels? But Jim was your grandfather."

"Ah, yes. But Jim was also a rogue, the rebel camel in the family."

Rebel camel? Wow, maybe you're really going crazy. Rebel camels, flying carpets and endless sand were not what you expected when you headed through the forest down Mystic Portal. You touch your head. Maybe you fell off your bike and hit it – that would explain things. But your fingers land on soft hair, not hard biking helmet. Something really peculiar has happened today.

Jamina stops braying. "Did you hear that?" she asks.

It's all quiet, you can't hear a thing. "What are you talking about?"

"The storm has stopped."

Putting the rest of your lunch in your backpack, you throw it on your shoulders and leap to your feet to unzip the tent.

"No," cries Jamina, but it's too late.

Sand pours through the doorway covering your legs to the knees. The sand is heavy, weighing you down. You struggle, but manage to clamber out of the tent.

Jamina's body is half submerged in red sand. Stumbling to her feet, she raises her haunches with her rear legs, causing an avalanche of sand to cascade over her shoulders, burying you to the waist.

"Why did you do that?" you cry, spitting grit from your teeth. Grabbing a few sips of water, you rinse your mouth, then struggle to the top of the sand.

Chuckling, she raises her front legs to stand. "Camels always get up with their rear legs first. It's just the way we're made." She stamps on the spot, flinging more sand over you, until she's compacted the sand beneath her.

Oh well, you'd better get the tent, in case there's another storm.

As you reach towards it, Jamina says, "Please stand out of the way." She places her jaws over the top of the tent, lifting it where the crossed poles meet. She tips it forward so the doorway is face down, and the sand pours out.

"Wow, you're handy! An excellent dromedary and great desert survival specialist."

She winks.

Soon you're back in her saddle, the tent tied behind you, traipsing across the desert.

After an hour of listening to more of Jamina's stories about her rebellious Grandpa, Jim, you reach the rise of a dune, and gasp.

Below is an oasis. A deep blue lake winks in the sunlight, surrounded by palms, bushes and low buildings the same color as the sand. At one end of the oasis stand brightly-striped tents with camels tethered nearby. A wide swathe of trampled sand surrounds the settlement, as if camels have been dancing around it. Dancing camels? That'll be the day.

Snorting, Jamina picks up her pace and starts running.

You're jostled from side to side, and hang on tight. She told you she could run forty miles per hour, but you had no idea it would feel like this. Your butt's being pummeled like a drum in a rock band, and your teeth clack like a row of tumbling dominoes. Sweat flies from your face as Jamina's hooves churn up sand behind you.

Stopping beside the tents, Jamina's sides heave. She folds her front knees to kneel, nearly tipping you off, but now wise to her ways, you grab the handle on the saddle, then dismount.

A bearded man wearing a white headscarf and loose red robes approaches. "Welcome home, Jamina." He pats her nose and she nuzzles his hand. "I see you've found a new rider who sits well in the saddle at high speed. Very well done. You're back just in time for the afternoon race."

Race? What race?

Oh! That wasn't a camel's dance floor surrounding the oasis. It was a race track.

The man extends his hand to you as a woman approaches. "I am Aamir, and this is my wife, Latifa. If you would like to stay and race Jamina in our camel race, you're welcome to stay with our family."

You gulp. That sprint on Jamina was crazy. It'll be a lot more dangerous racing with other camels.

"What will I do, if I don't race with Jamina?"

Aamir frowns, a thundercloud passing over his face.

Latifah shakes her head, as if urging you not to provoke him.

"My camel has been on a long journey to find you. She has rescued you from the perilous desert. We have offered you a new career as a camel racer and shelter in our tent. To refuse would be the height of rudeness. We would have to banish you from the oasis."

Banish? That means you'd have to leave. Maybe you'd find Tracey out there in the desert or another way to get back to Mystic Portal and your bike. Or maybe you'd get hopelessly lost.

It's time to make a decision. Do you:

Race Jamina in the camel races? **P206**

Or

Leave the oasis? **P126**

Encourage Jamina to run from the sandstorm

Although the sand stings, the main cloud is far away.

"Let's make a run for it," you yell to Jamina, clambering back into the saddle.

She rises and takes off, racing up a dune and plowing down the other side. Sand billows around her hooves as she runs. You're jolted from side to side. Your bones shudder.

Behind, the sandstorm is racing toward you, high above the dunes.

"Are you sure you don't want to pitch the tent?" Jamina asks.

Will she be fast enough to outrun the storm?

It's time to make a decision. Do you:

Pitch the tent to take shelter from the sandstorm? **P15**

Or

Keep Jamina running from the sandstorm? **P131**

Go with Tracey on the tatty flying carpet

"I'm sorry Jamina," you say. "Thanks for offering, but maybe I'll come to the oasis another time. Tracey is my friend so I should really help her."

"That's okay," says Jamina. "Let me help you get onto that thing."

"Here, take my hand," says Tracey. She leans down over the edge of the carpet, stretching her arm out towards you.

Jamina stands still so you can balance on her back. This is crazy. You never thought a mountain bike ride would have you balancing on a camel like an acrobat while trying to climb up to a swaying flying carpet. Grasping Tracey's hand firmly, you push off Jamina's back with your feet and Tracey yanks you onto the magic carpet.

"Have a good flight," calls Jamina as she turns and wanders off into the desert. Soon she's a tiny brown spot in the vast tundra of red.

Being on the carpet is like sitting on a bouncy castle. Every time you move, your weight makes the mat undulate in the air. "Whoa," you cry, "no wonder it's so hard to stay on this thing."

"You can say that again," says Tracey. "Riding a bike is much easier." She tugs a tassel and yells again, "Straight ahead, but steady!" The carpet swerves, nearly tipping her off.

You grab a handful of tassels and slide to the middle to save yourself from falling.

"You try," says Tracey. "This thing must be deaf. I'm yelling as loud as I can and it's not responding. Let's see if it likes your voice better."

Whenever someone yells at you, you never feel like doing what they're asking. Maybe yelling at the carpet isn't the key. Maybe you could try something different, like telling the carpet a joke.

No, that wouldn't work, because it wouldn't know what to do. Your teacher's always saying good manners open doors, whatever that means. Maybe talking nicely would change things.

Wind streams into your eyes as the carpet zips up into the air. It tilts, and you and Tracy start to slip off, your arms flailing. You both grab at stray threads. A loud ripping noise sends your heart thudding.

It's time to make a decision. Do you:

Yell at the magic carpet? **P26**

Or

Talk to the carpet politely? **P36**

Yell at the magic carpet

The hole in the carpet grows before your eyes. In a moment, you and Tracy will both be dumped on the sand, miles below. You'll break your arm, or your back, or something. Perhaps you'll both die.

"Stop!" You yell at the top your voice. "Stop or we'll die."

It works. The carpet screeches to a halt in midair. But the rip grows. With a tortured screech, the threads part and the carpet splits in two, Tracey holding one half, and you the other.

You both scream as you plummet through the air.

With twin whumps, you land on the side of a giant sand dune, letting go of the ragged pieces of mat as you land.

"Oof!"

"Ow!"

"Oh, no," moans Tracey, "there goes our transport!" She groans, shading her eyes as the carpet knits itself together and flies off. "Hey, come back!"

A faint laugh floats through the air.

Tracey turns to you. "There it is again. I could swear that thing was laughing at me the whole time it was trying to buck me off." She shakes her head and scrambles to her feet, brushing the sand off her bike shorts.

"It really did sound as if it was laughing," you say.

"Perhaps I should've told a joke after all. Or tried speaking politely. Did you try either?"

"No, I was too busy panicking. That's why I kept yelling." Tracey blushes. "What now?"

Still sitting, you fish through your backpack and pull out some water. "I think it's important to keep sipping water throughout the day, and to keep our heads shaded."

"Okay." Tracey takes a swig from her bottle and pulls a cap out of her backpack. "How will we ever get out of this desert?"

It doesn't look hopeful. Dunes surround you. That particular shade of red is beginning to get tiresome. And the sun is still doing overtime, working really hard to impress someone.

A loud snort startles you, making you jump. You whirl. It's Jamina, plodding over the crest of the dune, her broad feet stirring up puffs of sand as she walks.

"Here comes more transport," says Tracey. She points to Jamina, and yells, "Hey, you! Can you give us a ride?"

Elbowing Tracey aside, you mutter, "Stop yelling. Haven't you learned anything?" Your legs churn through the sand as you both make your way up to Jamina. "A sense of humor and some manners may come in handy. It's too late to try with the carpet, but there's no harm in trying with a talking camel."

You greet her. "Jamina, how wonderful to see you. It's

great you came to check up on us. Would you please give us a ride to the oasis?"

"I'm sorry, the oasis is in the other direction. I had to change my course to make sure you two were all right." Jamina bats her double row of eyelashes at you. "But I'd be delighted to give you a ride to an Arab merchant, only an hour or two from here."

"Thank you very much," you answer. "Jamina, I hadn't realized you had two sets of eyelashes above each eye."

"Helps keep the sand out. Now climb up and let's get going."

You sit on the seat over Jamina's hump, and Tracey sits on a brown bundle of cloth behind you. "What's this?" She asks.

"A tent for sandstorms," replies Jamina.

"Let's hope we don't get stuck in one of those." You shiver. "I read about a terrible sand storm in an adventure book, once. It sounded awful."

After a while, Jamina's rhythmic swaying and plodding make your head droop. A gentle snore comes from behind. Tracey's asleep already.

"Have a snooze too," says Jamina. "I'll wake you before we get there."

Despite trying desperately to stay awake, your eyelids close and you soon doze off.

Loud snorting wakes you. Turning her head, Jamina says, "Wake up sleepy heads, we're nearly there."

Behind you, Tracey groans. "My neck has a crick and my bottom's sore," she moans.

"At least you're alive," you say. "Better than being stranded in the desert by that silly carpet."

"Guess you're right," says Tracey. "Hey, camel, where are we?" She points to a wide building made of pale concrete. In the middle of the building is a domed roof. It's surrounded by sand, not another building in sight.

Elbowing Tracey, you whisper, "Her name is Jamina. Remember to speak politely to the camel or she may dump you in the desert too."

"Sorry," Tracey mumbles.

Jamina snorts and turns her head to wink at you. "You're right," she says. "Manners go a long way in the desert. Especially with merchant Karim. This is his home."

"Home? It looks more like a fortress."

Jamina lopes closer. The building is surrounded by a tall concrete wall. Guards pace along the top, at the ready.

"What are they guarding, Jamina?" asks Tracey.

"Merchant Karim grew up in poverty. He became rich through hard work and shrewd trading," Jamina says as you approach the gates. "He helps finance schools in the city slums, giving poor kids a chance to change their lives. He's a fair man, but tough."

As you draw closer, the flash of sunlight on binoculars

tells you that you're being watched.

"Desert bandits want a share of his riches. They're always breaking in to steal his gold and treasure, so merchant Karim hires guards to protect him." Jamina stops at the gate and a guard approaches.

"What is your business?" the guard asks Jamina.

"These two tourists have lost their way. I heard merchant Karim was hiring workers…"

What? Jamina's never said anything about you and Tracey working here. You shoot a worried glance at Tracey, but her eyes are glued to the guard's sharp sword.

"Ssh," she whispers.

She's probably right. It's best to stay quiet.

The guard looks over you and Tracey and says, "They look fit enough. Should be good workers. Follow me."

Jamina plods through the gate, following the guard. Once she's inside, she heads to the camel stables. After you dismount, the guard takes you through an arched doorway, down a wide corridor, to an enormous room.

A small man in yellow robes and blue headscarf greets you. "Aha, more workers?" He shakes hands with you and Tracey. "We have trouble with bandits attacking my home and preventing me from working with the poor," he says. "I need all the hands I can get. Are you willing to stay on as guards?"

"What would our duties be?" asks Tracey.

"Slingshots," answers the merchant. "We have long-range slingshots that shoot darts at the bandits' Land Rover tires, stopping them from attacking. We've found that young hands are much steadier at aiming slingshots than adults. What do you think?"

"We'll stay," says Tracey before you even have time to think, "if you can help us get home again."

"No problem. You've got a deal." Grinning, the merchant turns to his guards and they start a rapid conversation in Arabic.

You nudge Tracey, whispering, "Why did you agree to stay? You didn't even ask me."

"They have weapons," whispers Tracey. "We can always run away, if we want to."

Karim leads you out of the hallway and into the courtyard. "I'll take you to the training area so you can practice with slingshots," he says.

Before you get there, the massive gate to the compound slides open and a convoy of Land Rovers come inside. Drivers leap out of the vehicles and people rush from the building to help them unload their cargo.

"Ah, here are the supplies for my schools," says Karim. He disappears into the crowd to give a hand.

School supplies? No way. The boxes are labeled poison in large red letters, and skulls and crossbones are stamped on each one. "I don't trust him," you mutter to Tracey.

"Neither do I," she says. "It's now or never. Look, the

gate is still open. Shall we make a run for it, or stay?"

It's time to make a decision. Do you:

Run away from the merchant into the desert? **P33**

Or

Stay for slingshot training? **P192**

Run away from the merchant into the desert

"Let's go!" Grabbing Tracey's hand, you sneak towards the gate.

No one seems to notice you're leaving, not even the guards, who have come down from the wall to help unload the cargo. You both slip out the gate and run up the nearest dune.

"They'll see our tracks," says Tracey.

"Who cares? We just have to find a way back to Mystic Portal."

"How do we do that?" Tracey puffs as you head down the other side of the dune.

"Dunno, we'll think of something."

You race on into the desert, soon tiring. You share the last of the food and water from your backpacks, hiding behind a dune.

Tracey eyes the sun. "I've heard it's freezing in the desert at night," she says. "Do you have thermals with you?"

Tracey always thinks of good details when you plan a ride, so she'll have warm stuff with her. "Yeah, I usually bring extra gear when I go biking, but hopefully, we'll find a way home first."

"I'm tired," she says. "It's been a long day. Let's have a rest."

"Good idea. I'm bushed too." Using your backpacks

as pillows you both curl up on the sand and fall asleep.

A snort in your ear wakes you.

"Jamina? What are you doing here?"

"Merchant Karim sent me to save you. You'll die if you stay in the desert alone."

"But we want to get home to our families," says Tracey.

"He says if you come and help him, he'll help you get home. It's much better than dying here in the endless sand and heat."

You're parched and have no water left. Tracey nods. "Okay," you say. "We'll come and train to shoot slingshots, but after our first battle with the bandits we want to go home."

"Good," says Jamina. "Climb on my saddle and we'll get going."

Back at the compound, Karim welcomes you with open arms. "I was terrified bandits would catch you in the desert," he says. "Help me defeat them and I will get you home."

You and Tracey agree, and he takes you both across the courtyard towards a training area.

The gates slide open, allowing more four-wheel-drive vehicles in. Once again, the guards rush down from the walls and people come into the courtyard to help unload the cargo. Again, the boxes are labeled poison, but the merchant pretends they're supplies for schools.

Tracey nudges you. "Do you trust him?" she asks. "The gates are open we could run away, or we could stay for slingshot training. What you want to do?"

It's time to make a decision. Do you:

Run away from the merchant into the desert? **P33**

Or

Stay for slingshot training? **P192**

Talk to the carpet politely

"Oh, wonderful carpet," you call. "We're so grateful to be your passengers."

Nothing happens. The carpet rips further. Your hands slip on the loose threads you're clutching. It's a huge drop to the desert sand below.

"Please!" you shout. "Please, let us back on board."

Before your eyes, the tear in the carpet knits together and the far end swings around and hits you and Tracey on your bottoms. Flying through the air, you land sprawled in the middle of a golden swirl on the carpet's green background.

Tracey thuds down beside you. She must be stunned, because she hardly says a word.

That was close, but thankfully, nice manners did the trick.

The carpet floats smoothly through the air, the desert's warm breeze caressing your face. You lie back and relax, staring at the brilliant blue sky.

Then Tracey moans, "Dumb carpet. Wouldn't listen to a word I did. Stupid thing."

Instantly, the carpet bucks beneath you.

"Told you that carpet's dumb," she screams. "I hate it!" The carpet tilts. She slides over the edge, her legs in mid air.

You grab hold of her hands. "Stop it! The carpet only

listens when you're polite."

Her mouth hangs open and her eyebrows arch in astonishment. "W-what?"

She's getting heavier. Your arms ache from holding her. "You heard me. Oh great carpet, please forgive Tracey and let her back on board."

"Yes, please." Tracey's eyes light up. "I'm terribly sorry for my rudeness. I promise I won't do it again."

Tracey's side of the carpet lifts high into the air. She tumbles back on board, landing on top of you. She gasps, "Thank you, carpet. Thank you so much."

Was that faint tinkling sound the carpet laughing?

Grinning, you both lie back, gazing at the cloudless sky.

"This wasn't what I was expecting when we hit Camel Hump," Tracey says.

"Me neither. What a weird bike track. I had no idea Mystic Portal actually led to other worlds."

"Yeah, I guess each jump is some sort of portal," Tracey says. "Did you notice that the carpet is gold and green, just like my bike?"

"And the camel's saddle was the same colors as my bike."

"Intriguing."

After a while, faint noises float on the air. Sitting up, you spot some sand-red buildings and brightly-colored tents. "Look." You nudge Tracey.

"Some sort of settlement," she murmurs. "This should be interesting."

The carpet whisks you over the buildings, hovering above the tents. Below are striped awnings in all sorts of crazy color combinations. People sit on rugs with clay pots, food, crafts and trinkets spread out in front of them. Others are toasting peppers on metal skewers, the tantalizing aroma wafting through the air. Some are weaving. Children scamper between the stalls, laughing and calling to each other. Goats and camels are tethered on the far side of the marketplace. The bray of animals and the chatter of people bargaining rises above the busy market place.

"It's a bazaar," says Tracey.

"A what?"

"A Middle Eastern market. This is fantastic." She pats the carpet. "Thank you for bringing us here. Could we please get down?"

"Great that you asked politely," you say to her, "otherwise we'd be in for a bumpy landing."

The carpet drifts downwards and lands behind a tent. You and Tracey get off. The mat rolls itself up and tucks itself under Tracey's arm, shrinking until it's only a foot long. It looks like a wall hanging now, not a carpet. Amazing.

"Absolutely awesome." Tracey pats the carpet. "Thank you very much."

"Are you Tracey?" You ask. "Or a polite alien in Tracey's body?"

Tracey mock punches your arm. "Thank you!"

You're making your way between the tents to the marketplace when a girl pops her head out of a tent flap. "Hello," she says in accented English, "is that a magic carpet?"

"Maybe," says Tracey, protectively tucking the carpet behind her back.

"Do you want to trade?" asks the girl. She ducks back into the tent and steps outside a moment later, holding a tarnished gold lamp. "This lamp is the home of a magic genie. If you polish it, the genie will grant you three wishes."

Wow, a genie! Three magic wishes! You could wish for anything you want, new bikes for all of you, a way to get home, and a custom-built mountain bike track in your own backyard.

Tracey's eyes are shining. No doubt she's imagining all the things she wants. "Do we each get three wishes?"

"Sure," says the girl.

"Hang on," barks Tracey. "If you can wish for anything you want, why don't you have a magic carpet already?"

"Um…" The girl's eyes slide away, and then she smiles, as if she's just come up with a good idea. "Because I've already used my wishes," she says, flashing her white teeth. "Now it's your turn. Do you want to trade the carpet for the lamp and genie?"

It's time to make a decision. Do you:

Trade the magic carpet for the lamp and genie? **P178**

Or

Keep the magic carpet and go to the bazaar? **P41**

Keep the magic carpet and go to the bazaar

You and Tracey glance at each other. There's something not quite right about what the girl said. "Um, no thanks," you say. "We need to go to the market."

"I can guide you around the bazaar and make sure no one rips you off," she says.

"Sure, that'll be great. I'm Tracey. What's your name?" asks Tracey.

"Daania."

"That's a pretty name," says Tracey, taking the girl's hand and heading towards the bazaar.

"It means beautiful." Daania says.

Even though Tracey's learned some manners on this trip, she's forgotten to introduce you. You trail behind them, your stomach rumbling as the scent of delicious food tickles your nostrils.

"Let's get something to eat," says Tracey.

"Just what I was thinking," you say. "What's good?"

Daania leads you to a stand. "This is my mother." A lady, wearing a brightly covered headscarf, smiles at you and thrusts some round bread towards you. "Her olive flatbread is the best in the bazaar. It's from my grandmother's secret recipe." Daania holds up flatbread smothered in olives and crumbly cheese. "I milk the goats and make the cheese myself."

"That's cool," you say.

"Cold?" asks Daania, obviously confused. "No, the milk is usually warm when it comes straight from the goat."

"Cool means good," you explain.

"Really? That's odd," she says.

"How much is the bread?" asks Tracey.

"As much bread as you can eat for a ride on your carpet," says Daania, eyeing the small mat still tucked under Tracey's arm.

Daania seems awfully keen on that carpet. Once she gets on it, who knows if she'll return.

Tracey must be thinking the same thing, because she says, "Let's all eat first, then go for a ride together once we've looked around.

"A good idea," says Daania, handing you the warm bread.

The goat's cheese is tangy and the flatbread is spicy, so Daania offers you both a drink of goat's milk, which tastes really strong.

Tracey wrinkles her nose as she drinks, but says, "Thank you."

You grin. This new polite Tracey is much better than the old Tracey, who was always fun, but often complained.

Munching on a handful of dates from Daania's mother, you and Tracey follow Daania around the bazaar, past rugs laden with nuts, seeds, dates, figs, olives and oranges. People wave and call out to you. A goat follows Tracey, butting her from behind.

"Stupid thing. Why is it butting me?"

"It likes you," says Daania. "If you ignore her, she'll keep butting your bottom. If you're nice to her, she'll stop."

Seems like there are a lot of lessons about being nice, here, in the desert. You try not to smile as Tracey bends down to pat the goat behind the ears. The animal bleats and licks Tracey's hand, then runs off between some tents.

"You've made a new friend," Daania says.

Tracey beams.

A man calls out, waving a beaded necklace and gesturing at bright strings of glass beads hanging under his yellow and red striped awning. "Nice for you," he calls to Tracey. "Nice necklet."

She smiles at his incorrect pronunciation and agrees. "Yes, very nice."

"You want to buy?"

"No thank you," she says politely.

Suddenly the roar of a motor fills the air. A Land Rover, with a red skull emblazoned on the bonnet, screeches through a gap in the tents. Churning up sand with its wheels, it races into the marketplace crushing produce and crafts and scattering people and animals. Men jump out of the vehicle, armed with long swords.

One of them is splattered in pink paint.

Very odd.

"Bandits," says Daania urgently. "Quick, run!"

She tugs you and Tracey behind a tent and whirls to face Tracey. "The carpet. It's our only chance of escape."

Flinging the carpet onto the ground, Tracey says, "Please, carpet, help us get away."

The carpet unfurls, expanding to full size, and hovers just above the ground. The three of you leap on and take off past the tents. People are yelling, wailing and flinging pots and pans at the bandits. A chicken squawks, flapping past you.

Tracey ducks as a copper saucepan zips past her head. "Higher please, carpet, higher. We don't want them to hit you!"

Warm wind whistles past you as the carpet gains altitude, rising above the tents, zooming away from the hurly-burly of the bazaar and out over the desert.

"I fear for your safety if we return," says Daania. "These bandits create havoc and steal things, but they don't usually hurt us. I have heard that they sometimes kidnap foreigners to work in a factory. Up ahead is a way to get to your homeland, or we could return. What do you want to do?"

You glance at Tracey, but she just looks scared. "I dunno," she says in a small voice. "Up to you."

There's sand and blue sky ahead or bandits behind.

It's time to make a decision. Do you:
Fly the magic carpet straight ahead to get home? **P174**
Or
Return to the bazaar? **P145**

Bypass Camel Hump and go down the chicken line

"Not today, Tracey," you call, hoping she can hear you, even though she's out of sight. "I'm off to Ogre Jaws." Turning your handlebars, you go down the chicken line – the narrow trail leading around the jump that meets up with the main track further on

Even the chicken line is challenging, with gnarly roots and steep drops through tangled brush. Branches swipe at your face. You duck, just missing them. Twisting around a tree trunk and scraping under a branch, you spot the flash of Sidney's orange bike ahead of you.

He leaps a log, still making chicken noises, and lands with a thunk, zooming down the trail.

You crow like rooster, and jump the log too. If you're going to skip Camel Hump and be a chicken, you might as well be a funky chicken. You, Tracey and Sidney have always made a great game out of taking chicken lines. Not that Tracey takes them that often. With her new bike, she can conquer most jumps easily, and, you have to admit, she also has mean skills.

You shoot out onto the main track again. Sidney rounds the berm, disappearing around the corner. You follow. He rides over a small rise and gets air. He clears the jump by at least a yard.

"How much air did you get?" calls Sidney.

"About a half a yard," you yell, "but you easily got a

whole yard."

"Yahoo!" he yells in triumph. "I'm taking the next jump."

After walking Mystic Portal, you know what's coming. You whizz around the corner, your back tire sliding in the dirt.

Sidney has stopped in the middle of the track.

You slam on your brakes and skid past him, churning up leaf litter and narrowly missing his bike. "Hey! Are you crazy? We nearly had a smash up." Your heart's pounding.

Sidney's staring at the track, shaking his head. "Something weird is going on."

"Yeah! You're trying to kill us!"

Frowning, Sidney points at the track. "Where's Dino Drop? It's disappeared."

He's right. When you walked down here recently, there was a giant redwood across the track, carved into a stegosaurus. To get to the drop, bikers had to go under the stegosaurus. But now it's gone.

"St-raaaange…" How could it have disappeared? "Perhaps someone took the stegosaurus away?" Even as you say it, you know that's not right, because the drop jump is no longer there.

"Do you think someone filled in the drop with dirt and covered it with dead leaves and pine needles?" Sidney sounds like he doesn't believe a word he's saying.

"Doubt it. Maybe we've just forgotten the track. It could be around the next corner." But all the times you've ridden with Sidney, he's always remembered every track – each jump, gap, corner, drop off and bridge. You shrug. "Nothing we can do, except keep riding."

"Yeah, I guess." He glances around again. "Where's Tracey? I haven't seen her since Camel Hump."

"Maybe she went down a different track."

"There wasn't a different track when we walked it," says Sidney, stubbornly. "How could there suddenly be one today?"

"Dunno," you reply. "This is really odd. Maybe she's ahead of us."

"Yeah, we'd better catch up." Sidney pushes off on his pedals and rides down the narrow trail.

Leaves flick into your face as the downhill track winds through a bushy area. The trail flattens, heading between groves of towering pines, then you face a short uphill climb. Legs pumping, you hammer the pedals, grunting as you mount the incline. You sigh in relief when you get to the crest. A whoosh of air escapes you as you zoom after Sidney down the hill.

Sidney breaks out of the trees and shoots over a pile of bark chips onto a grassy slope. The next huge jump is visible at the end of the clearing, just before the trail enters the forest again. A crudely painted sign sticks out of the grass: *Ogre Jaws*. It's a gap jump. The first dirt ramp will spit you into the air above a pit of jagged chunks of old porcelain, shaped like monster's teeth. You have to clear the toothy gap and land your bike on the downward ramp on the other side. On either side of the downward ramp are huge mosaic eyes, like an ogre's. Whoever designed this jump has a wild imagination.

With a whoop, Sidney races up the ramp and is airborne, high above the jagged teeth. In a flash of red, he disappears, vanishing in midair like Tracey did.

Freaky.

Maybe you should follow him and see what happens. Maybe you'll have a great adventure, but it looks dangerous. Something could go wrong. Who knows where Sidney is. And Tracey. You haven't seen her since Camel Hump.

In a moment you'll be at the turn off to the chicken line.

It's time to make a decision. Do you:

Hit Ogre Jaws? **P50**

Or

Bypass Ogre Jaws and go down the chicken line? **P93**

Hit Ogre Jaws

Moments after deciding to take the jump, you're airborne, high above those menacing porcelain teeth. Wind rushes into your face, making you grin. It'll be no problem to clear the jump and land on the other side. You brace yourself for landing.

But that's not what happens.

Suddenly, the earth cracks open like an enormous mouth and a long red tongue whips out from between Ogre Jaws. The tongue wraps itself around the bike frame and your leg, and yanks you downwards.

The tongue releases you, leaving a slimy trail of goo over your leg. Gripping your handlebars, you plummet through darkness. With a soft whump, you land. That's odd, your bike seems to bend as it lands, as if it's made of rubber, not steel. Weird, because your suspension isn't that good and normally rattles your bones during landings.

Your bike keeps moving forwards through the dark, although the sound of its tires has changed. Something fluffy tickles your legs. You take a hand off the handlebars, and touch the frame. *It's fluffy*. Perhaps some mossy tree roots got stuck around the bike as you fell. You feel along the frame and up the stem towards the handlebars. Nope, not roots. Definitely fluffy.

Your bike goes over a lump in the ground and lurches.

Green light beams out from your headlamp illuminating a dirt tunnel festooned with tree roots. Wait, your headlamp emits white light, not green. And it's in your backpack, not mounted on your bike.

Goosebumps break out on your arms and a cold trickle of sweat runs down your neck. Something creepy is going on. Where's Sidney?

"Sidney!" you holler.

The bike trills beneath you. "What is Sidney?"

What? The bike's talking to you? "H-he's m-my friend," you stutter.

"Aha, the other human!" a chirpy voice replies. "I think Bog the ogre got him."

"Bog the ogre?" Your voice shakes as you answer. Your bike is talking to you. Are you going mad?

The green light swivels from side to side, as if it's searching for something. Light catches on the handlebars which aren't handlebars at all. You're holding horns protruding from an orange furry head.

You're riding a one-eyed monster that beams green light from its eye.

Swallowing hard, you try to speak, but only a squeak comes out. "Eep."

"Bog likes human-toast for breakfast," sings the monster, still racing along the dark tunnel with its bright-green eye beam flickering over the walls. "He plunges a fork through the middle of the human and toasts it over fire. Says it's his favorite snack. Can't say I've ever tried human, but, then again, I'm vegetarian."

"G-glad to hear you're v-vegetarian," you reply. "P-please, wh-who are you?"

"I am Sharmeena, a track-keeper," the furry creature replies. "Track-keepers look after Mystic Portal."

"Wh-where are we g-going?"

"Why, to rescue your friend," says the track-keeper. "What was his name? Sidney?"

"Um, yeah, Sidney." You try to swallow the lump in your throat again, but it won't budge.

"You do want to save your friend, don't you?" she chirps.

Of course you do, but you'll have to face an ogre that toasts kids for breakfast! "Um… sure."

"You don't sound that sure," says the track-keeper. "If you want, I can save him myself, and leave you here, but if you choose that, I can't guarantee your safety."

It's time to make a decision. Do you:

Go with Sharmeena to save Sidney from Bog the ogre? **P53**

Or

Stay in the tunnel on your own? **P56**

Go with Sharmeena to save Sidney from Bog the ogre

"Of course I'll save Sidney," you reply. "He's a good friend. I'd never let him down."

"Hold on tight," calls Sharmeena.

She races down the tunnel, leaping over tree roots and flying through the air. This track-keeper is as good as a mountain bike – except she has four legs and you have no control over where you're going.

"Bog's lair is in a cave along here," Sharmeena says. "Keep your eyes peeled, in case we miss the entrance."

Wrapping your arms around her neck, you lean low with your chin on the track-keeper's head, peering out over the orange fur between her horns. The eerie green light from Sharmeena's eye flashes over the walls. Her hooves thud along the ground.

"There's an opening ahead," you call in a hoarse whisper, pointing at a yellow glow coming from a fissure in the tunnel wall.

Sharmeena slows and creeps along the passage, hugging the walls. Rumbling drifts down the tunnel, getting louder as you approach the cave entrance. The light from the track-keeper's eye dims, until you're plunged into darkness, except for that unusual yellow light ahead.

Your heart thuds. Sharmeena cranes her neck around the wall and you peer into the mouth of the cave. In the yellow glow of a lantern, an enormous ogre with a red Mohawk lies stretched on the floor, his snores rumbling through the cave – Bog.

Behind Bog, in a flimsy-looking cage, is Sidney.

Sidney's eyes light up when he sees you, but he holds a finger to his lips, cautioning you to be quiet, and points at Bog with his other hand.

Still riding Sharmeena, you creep into Bog's lair, around the sleeping ogre. A stench wafts from Bog's feet, making you pinch your nose. Foot odor deluxe. No way you want to breathe that in.

When you're out of the stink-zone, near Sidney's cage, you hop off your new orange-furred friend.

"Boy, am I glad to see you," Sidney whispers. "Can you get me out of here?"

"This is my friend Sharmeena, a track-keeper. We've come to rescue you," you whisper. "These bars don't look very strong. We should be able to bend them in no time."

The track-keeper turns her single luminous-green eye towards you. Her pupil is a swirling spiral, which focuses on you, as she leans over and whispers, "Be careful. The bars are trickier than they look."

"Bog told me the bars were dangerous," says Sidney. "He used a key on one of these." He points at a row of locks on the door of the cage.

"Fat lot of good a key will do us, if Bog has it," you

say, reaching for the bars. "I don't want to wake him up."

"No. Listen!" Sidney says. "That gold thing glinting under his head is the key. All you have to do is move his head while he's sleeping and slide the key out. Then I'm free. No risk, that way, see? Not like the bars."

"No risk?" you hiss. "What about my hand while I'm trying to move his head? Or my arm? I quite like having hands, thanks. I'll take my chances with the bars."

Sharmeena flicks her orange tail back and forth like a wary cat. "The bars are dangerous," she says. "Be careful."

"Why? What happens when you try to bend them?"

"Whenever humans touch the bars, they're never the same again," the track-keeper says. The spiral in the middle of her eye swirls faster, as if she's panicking.

It's time to make a decision. Do you:

Try to use Bog's key? **P57**

Or

Bend the bars to free Sidney? **P81**

Stay in the tunnel on your own

The tunnel is creepy, but being pierced with a fork and toasted has got to be worse.

Yawning loudly, you stretch. "Um, I'm quite tired. Perhaps I should rest here, while you save Sidney."

That should sort things out nicely. Sidney will be saved by Sharmeena and you won't risk your life facing Bog.

The track-keeper stops suddenly, throwing you headfirst over her horns into a heap on the tunnel floor.

You slam into a mass of tree roots. "Ow! What did you do that for?"

Sharmeena turns her gaze on you in a flood of green light. Her eye is luminous green with a swirling spiral at the centre. "Are you sure you want to me to save him and leave you here?" There's a touch of scorn in her voice.

It's time to make a decision. Do you:

Go with Sharmeena to save Sidney from Bog the ogre? **P53**

Or

Stay in the tunnel? **P116**

Try to use Bog's key

"If I get hurt touching the bars then we're both stuck, so I'm going to try the key."

"Good idea." Sidney sighs in relief. "If you touched them, I was worried something awful would happen."

Sharmeena nods. "You would've have transformed into a creature. Most humans react badly when it happens."

"Thanks for warning me." You grin. "I'm quite happy as a human."

Bog gives a loud splutter in his sleep, then his rumbling snores continue to echo around the cave. The golden key glints under his left ear.

"The key's right under Bog's head. If I touch him, he'll wake up and eat us." You scratch your head. "There's got to be another way. Can you think of anything, Sidney?"

"You could tickle him so he moves," suggests Sidney, "then snatch the key."

"And get snapped up in those giant jaws when he wakes up?" You shake your head. "No way. But you're right, we need him to move so I can grab it."

Bog farts. A creeping purple haze spreads from beneath his bottom out along the floor. A rotten-egg stench threatens to overwhelm you.

"Whatever you do, do it quick." Sharmeena coughs. "Those farts are toxic. I can't stand them much longer."

The ogre's belly grumbles in his sleep. He's hungry. You have to move fast before he wakes up for toasted Sidney.

Bog's stomach growls again, like a prowling tiger.

That's it! You can use his hunger! You snatch a cookie out of your backpack and approach Bog's head.

"That'll never work," says Sidney. "He's way too hungry to only eat a cookie. If you wake him, he'll just snap down the cookie, and then have us for main course."

Sharmeena pipes up, "And me for desert."

You place your finger on your lips to hush your friends. Leaning over Bog's head, you hold the chocolate chip cookie above his nose.

"Snaarrck." Bog gives an enormous snore.

You twitch, dropping the cookie in surprise.

With fingers like lightning, you snatch it before it hits Bog's face – luckily, your reflexes are fast.

The scent of chocolate chip wafts towards you. Bog's nostrils flare, quivering as he takes in the aroma. Gradually, you move the cookie towards his right ear. Bog turns his head, his nose following the delicious scent.

The stem of the giant key is poking out from under Bog's head. You grasp the stem with your left hand, but it won't budge. You'll have to move the cookie further so Bog will move his head and free the key. Leaning over Bog's face, you stretch your arm as far as you can.

Oh, no, your sleeve brushes his nose!

Bog snorts and rolls his head, trapping your left hand. Oily green wax dribbles out of Bog's ear, running onto your hand and the floor. Blech! It stinks. Odd brown blobs fleck the greasy wax. Ooh, gross, they're dead insects. You wrinkle your nose.

Gently, you try to remove your hand. Bog snarls in his sleep. There's no way you can pull your hand out, or you'll wake him.

In his cage, Sidney grimaces and his eyes grow wide. The track-keeper steps towards the cave wall and seems to melt against the rock until she disappears. Cool magic, but how are you and Sidney going to escape this mess?

You could yell and startle Bog so he moves, and then dash out of the cave – but that would leave Sidney with an angry ogre. Or you could try with the cookie again.

Leaning over Bog's head again, you dangle the cookie in front of his nose. As soon as his nostrils twitch, you move the cookie away. His nose and head follow. In moments, you've pulled your sticky hand out from under his head. The golden key is safe in your grip.

You yank the cookie away, but Bog lets out a vicious snarl and his eyelids flutter. Beads of sweat break out on your forehead. In a desperate move, you toss the cookie into his mouth and dash over to Sidney's cage. Munching in his sleep, Bog finishes the cookie in seconds, then starts snoring again.

"Phew, that was close," whispers Sidney. "Which lock?"

The track-keeper's orange fur gradually emerges from the rock. "How did you do that?" Sidney asks her. "You disappeared."

"It's just camouflage," she replies.

"Just?" says Sidney. "Imagine the tricks we could play on Tracey, using camouflage like that on our bike tracks."

"Stop fooling around." You wave the key. "Which lock does this key work on?"

"Dunno," says Sidney.

Your heart is still pounding. You've just risked your life. "Not helpful," you snap.

The track-keeper interrupts before the two of you start a full-on argument. "The keys works on all the locks, but only one will open the cage. The rest are enchanted."

That news makes you want to scream, but you don't dare – you might wake Bog.

"Look this one has a lightning show going on." Sidney points at a silver lock with traces of blue light flickering across its surface.

Sharmeena backs away from it. "That's a powerful enchantment." Her eye swirls.

"This one's got camels on it," you point at a brass lock with tiny engraved camels around the base.

"And that one has dolphins," says Sharmeena, nodding at a lock encrusted with green, as if it's been pulled out of a sunken ship.

"What about this rusty old lock?" you ask. "Did he use this one when he locked you up?

"Sorry," Sidney says. "I don't know. He threw me into the cage and locked it up before I had a chance to see."

It's time to make a decision. Which of the four locks will you try with the key?

Try the silver lock with blue flashes? **P62**

Try the brass lock engraved with camels? **P64**

Try the green-encrusted lock with dolphins on it? **P68**
Or

Try the plain rusty lock? **P72**

Try the silver lock with blue flashes

"This one looks the most exciting." You grab the lock. A buzz shoots through your fingers. You drop it, shaking your hand.

"What?" says Sidney. "Did it hurt you?"

"Not really. It just gave me a fright."

Sharmeena nudges your elbow with her nose, her eye whirling rapidly. "Careful."

You grip the lock again.

A buzz runs through your hand, making your arm tingle all the way to your elbow. There's no way you're letting magic get the better of you. You have to free Sidney.

It takes a moment to get used to the weird sensation running up your arm.

"You okay?"

Sidney's eyes are doing that wide thing again. He looks like he has a couple of saucers in his head instead of eyeballs.

"Yeah, I'm fine." Well, almost.

You raise the key towards the lock, but before you insert it, blue light zaps between the lock and the key, crackling, and making your other hand buzz and your ears tingle. You gasp, but hold the lock and key firm.

"Watch out!" calls Sidney. "You have blue sparks in your hair."

It's time to make a decision. Do you:
Go ahead despite the sparks? **P119**
Or
Choose a different lock? **P80**

Try the brass lock engraved with camels

"This one looks interesting." You finger the heavy brass lock.

"I like camels," says Sidney. "We should try it."

Behind you, the ogre groans in his sleep and turns over.

If only Bog had rolled over before – you could have snatched the key without getting your hand covered in greasy earwax.

"Be quick," says Sharmeena.

As you bring the key towards the lock, your skin grows warm. Sweat beads upon your forehead, as if you're sunbathing on a baking summer's day. Something snorts.

You whirl. But only Bog and the track-keeper are behind you. "What was that?"

"Sounded like a camel," said Sidney. "I heard one at the zoo last week and it was just the same."

Turning the lock over, you examine it. You could swear the position of the camels has changed. Surely they were walking in a straight line around the bottom of the lock before? Now they're heading upwards, towards the keyhole. "Look. Has this changed?"

Sidney peers at the lock. "Maybe. Nah, that's not possible." He blows out his breath in frustration. "Dunno. Are you going to get me out of here?"

"Hurry, Bog will be awake soon." Sharmeena's eye

whirls. She's worried.

It's time to make a decision. Do you:
Turn the key in the camel lock? **P66**
Or
Choose a different lock? **P80**

Turn the key in the camel lock

The warm sunny sensation that this lock radiates sure beats waiting in an underground tunnel with an ogre who wants to eat you.

"Let's go for it." You shrug. "We've got nothing to lose."

"Famous last words," says Sidney as you turn the key in the lock.

In a flash of blinding white light, you and Sidney are suddenly back on Mystic Portal on your bikes.

"Thanks," calls Sidney, "I couldn't have got away from Bog without you."

"All good," you call.

Tracey is further down the track in front of you. Sidney races behind her on his hard tail. Sharmeena is galloping along next to you as you ride.

"It's been great meeting you." She grins. "Well done saving Sidney from Bog. But now I have to go. Track maintenance is calling."

"Bye," you call.

Her orange fur flashes between the trees, and then she's gone.

Track maintenance? What did she mean? Surely she's not the mysterious Mystic Portal track builder? How could a four-legged creature hold a spade, carve trees or sculpt rock? You pedal hard to catch up with the others.

Tracy takes a corner and Sidney follows. You zip around the corner, then speed down the track.

Ahead, the trail splits in two. It looks familiar. Deja vu! There's that makeshift sign with the badly painted camel that you saw at the beginning of the track.

"I'm taking Camel Hump," calls Tracey.

"I'm taking the chicken line!" Sidney clucks like a chicken, then turns left to bypass the jump. He disappears into the trees.

Tracey swings to the right. "Woohoo! Camel Hump, here I come." Her bike crunches through gravel on way down the hill to the jump. "Coming?" she calls. She wooshes up the steep reddish rise of Camel Hump. Her bike flies into the air. She disappears.

No, that can't be right. You must be mistaken. She must've landed beyond your line of vision.

You're nearly at the fork in the trail. To your right is Camel Hump. To your left is the way out – the chicken line.

It's time to make a decision. You have 3 choices. Do you:

Go back and choose another lock? **P80**

Hit Camel Hump? **P6**

Or

Bypass Camel Hump and go down the chicken line? **P46**

Try the green-encrusted lock with dolphins on it

"Try that one," suggests Sidney. "It looks interesting."

"I think so too." You reach out and cradle the chunky lock in your hand. It's heavy. Bits of green debris break off, revealing engravings of seahorses, turtles and more dolphins.

"Very beautiful." Sharmeena peers over your shoulder. "A good choice."

"It's like an underwater world," you murmur.

You insert the key in the lock. Cold washes over you. Your ears are filled with the whoosh of the sea.

"What's that?" Sidney's eyes are huge again.

"Could you hear it too?"

"I did as well," says the track-keeper.

Behind you, Bog yawns and stretches in his sleep.

"Quick, he's waking up. Get me out of here. Please," Sidney begs.

It's time to make a decision. Do you:

Turn the key in the dolphin lock? **P69**

Or

Choose a different lock? **P80**

Turn the key in the dolphin lock

Bog stirs, rolling over and muttering.

"Quick," whispers Sharmeena. "Now."

You turn the key in the dolphin lock. The whooshing grows, vibrating in your ears. Your vision goes blue. The cage door flies open and all three of you are propelled through the air.

Bog leaps to his feet, roaring, "No! My toast is running away!"

In a flash of blue light, Bog and the tunnels disappear.

You and Sidney are on your bikes going down Mystic Portal, with Sharmeena running beside you.

"Congratulations on choosing a good lock," she calls, veering off the track. "Now that you're safe from Bog, I have to go. Track maintenance is calling."

"Bye," you call, as her orange fur disappears into the trees.

"Track maintenance? Is that what track-keepers do?" asks Sidney.

"Hey, there's Tracey. Let's catch up with her."

You race down the track behind Tracey and Sidney and come to a loop heading across a stream. You pass a sign: *Dolphin Slide.*

"Great to see you guys," yells Tracey. "Let's jump!" She zips up a rock shaped like a dolphin, and leaps off the top, over the stream. Tracey and her bike disappear.

"Here we go again," calls Sidney. His bike sploshes through a puddle, up the rock. He jumps and vanishes.

Your tires hiss against the wet rock as you shoot up over Dolphin Slide.

In a flash of blue light, the trail and trees are gone. You're riding on a dolphin through the ocean. Sidney and Tracey are riding dolphins too. The sun slants through the watery blue. An orange octopus floats past, waving its tentacles, then disappears into a mass of green seaweed nestled in a bank of colorful coral. Light wink among the coral, casting a yellow glow. What are they? Underwater glow worms?

"Wow," says Tracey. "Can you believe this? It's incredible."

"Hey, we can talk underwater." Bubbles rise from Sidney's mouth as he speaks. "And breathe."

"Amazing. What's next?" you ask.

"I thought you'd never ask," says the dolphin you're riding on.

"Squee," replies Tracey's dolphin, "let's tell them."

Talking dolphins? Wow.

"Welcome to the underwater portion of Mystic Portal," your dolphin says. "My name is Squee, leader of this pod. We're your hosts, today, but you won't just be riding us. In order to get back to Mystic Portal, you need to compete in a race or take a tour. You can choose to ride seahorses in the Round the Coral Peninsula

Extravaganza race, or go by turtleback on a Terrific Turtle Tour and see all the underwater sights."

"Cool." Bubbles tickle your nose as you speak. "What do you guys want to do?"

Sidney's eyes are shining. "I'm all for racing. The Round the Coral Peninsula Extravaganza by seahorse is for me."

Tracey's grinning. "I've always wanted to dive, so I'm going on a Terrific Turtle Tour to see all the underwater sights."

"Sounds good," says Squee, swimming under a coral bridge. "What will it be for you?"

It's time to make a decision. Do you:

Ride a seahorse in the Round the Coral Peninsula Extravaganza? **P97**

Or

Ride a turtle on a Terrific Turtle Tour? **P108**

Try the plain rusty lock

The dolphin lock, camel lock and the lock that's flashing electric blue all look like they're enchanted. Maybe it's safer to go with a normal-looking rusty lock. But it wouldn't harm to inspect them all again before you try.

You raise your key, hovering over the electric blue lock. A tingle goes up your arm. Is that a good sign? Hard to tell.

As you touch the dolphin lock, your body goes cold and roaring fills your ears. Odd. Your fingers graze the camel lock, and you instantly feel warm. When you handle the rusty lock, nothing happens.

"I think I'll go for this one," you tell Sidney, putting your key into the rusty keyhole. Flakes of orange rust fall to the floor, the same shade as the track-keeper's fur.

Bog groans in his sleep.

"Quick," Sharmeena says, "I think he's waking up."

Sidney shakes his head. "The rusty one is the plainest of all. Surely Bog wouldn't have chosen normal lock to keep me in here."

Bog's murmuring. You must be quick.

It's time to make a decision. Do you:

Turn the key in the rusty lock? **P73**

Or

Choose a different lock? **P80**

Turn the key in the rusty lock

Bog snarls in his sleep. His eyes are still closed, but at this rate, they won't be for long.

With a flick of your wrist, you turn the key in the lock, but it's stuck and won't turn the whole way.

"It's jammed," you whisper. "I can't turn it."

"It can't be the right lock then," Sidney says. "Hurry up, choose another one."

Bog stomach rumbles. "Hungry, hungry," he mutters in his sleep. "Make toast."

You twist the key again, but it won't budge. "It's too stiff. If I only I had some oil..."

Bog thrashes on the floor, then stretches and burps.

Maybe, just maybe, the ogre's grossness could be useful.

In a shower of rusty flakes, you yank the key out of the lock and race over to Bog. Bending, you dip the key in the patch of his greasy earwax. As you run back to the cage, the gold key shines in the lantern light, slick with oil.

"This should do the trick." You jam the key into the lock and turn it. Stuck. Again.

"Try again." Sharmeena urges.

Sidney's breath is rasping. His eyes are fixed on Bog, who lets out a giant fart that makes Sharmeena cough.

"Wassat?" Bog mutters in his sleep.

You jiggle the key in the lock, trying to turn it. It clanks against the bars.

"My toast!" Bog's bellow makes you jump.

"He's awake." Sidney's pale and trembling. "Run. Save yourselves," he hisses.

Frantically, you give the key one last twist. The lock springs open. Sidney's cage door swings ajar. He scrambles out of the cage, knocking you over.

"Hop on," cries Sharmeena.

Sidney leaps upon her back and reaches down, pulling you up to sit in front of him.

"No! Mine!" Bog roars, "I want toast!" He shoots a jet of flame from his jaws towards you.

Sharmeena springs through the air above the flame, with you and Sidney clinging to the fur on her back.

But Bog dashes to the entrance, blocking it with his enormous body. His loincloth swings as he stamps his foot. "Not fair! I'm hungry!" His bellows make the cave shake. A rock falls from the ceiling, narrowly missing you, showering you with dirt. "My food." He waves an angry arm at Sidney and opens his mouth, about to blast you with flame.

You have to think fast. "Stop, Bog."

He stares at you, startled.

There must be something you can do to stop him from making toast out of you all.

"I'm scared," Sidney whispers. He's squeezing your

waist so tight, he's making something in your backpack crinkle.

That's it! Your backpack.

"Bog, you're hungry, right?"

"Yes, eat toast." A tendril of smoke curls from his lips. He smiles. "Eat toast. Two human toasts. Now." He opens his mouth wide, showing a great set of teeth.

"Bog, have you ever tried potato chips?" you ask. "They're much tastier than human toast." You click your fingers and hold them up above your shoulder. Sidney unzips your backpack and passes you a packet of potato chips.

You open them and hold them out to Bog.

Warily he approaches, sniffing the air. He snatches the pack and tosses the chips into his open mouth, wrapper and all.

"Yucky," he snarls, spitting out bits of wrapper. "Human tricked me."

"Peanut butter and jelly?"

Sidney shoves your sandwich into your hands. Unwrapping it first, you smile and hold it on your extended palm.

This time Bog approaches, snarling and gnashing his teeth. "If this no good, I blast you all." Bog stomps back to the entrance with the sandwich, sniffing it with narrowed eyes.

Holding your breath, you watch Bog nibble your

sandwich.

Behind you, Sidney's rummaging in his backpack. He taps your shoulder and passes you his own peanut butter and jelly sandwich.

"Hold on tight," whispers Sharmeena. "We'll make a run for it. Keep your faces down so he doesn't burn them."

Bog swallows your sandwich. His eyes light up. He beams at you. "Much better than human toast," he says. "You give me more, I let you go." His eyes land on Sidney's sandwich in your hand. He licks his lips.

"Not so fast, Bog," you say.

"Why not?" hisses Sidney in your ear. "Let's get out of here."

Bog eyes up Sidney's sandwich. "Want it, NOW." He's about to have an ogre-sized tantrum. He could cause a cave in. You could all be buried alive.

"If I give you this sandwich and teach the track-keepers how to make you more peanut butter and jelly, do you promise not to hurt them anymore?"

"Never wanted hurt them," says Bog. "Just hungry. Very grumpy when hungry.

"Really? Is that all?" Sharmeena says. "We track-keepers never realized. We'd be happy to feed you peanut butter and jelly when you're hungry. But please, let us know before you're starving and grumpy."

"No problem." Bog toasts the last piece of Sidney's

sandwich with a puff of flame. He pops it in his mouth, then burps. "Thanks for feeding me," he says. "See you soon."

He waves as Sharmeena leaps through the cave entrance back into the tunnel with you and Sidney on her back.

Away from Bog's lantern, the tunnel is pitch black. Sharmeena lights the way with the green beam from her eye. Soon she's racing along the tunnel, leaping up the sides and bounding back down to the floor again.

"This beats any mountain bike ride," calls Sidney, still clutching your waist.

"It's awesome," you reply. "Mystic Portal's my new favorite trail."

You race along the tunnel for a few minutes, your adrenaline pumping and the breeze rushing into your face. Sharmeena skids to a halt. There's a fork in the tunnel.

"Thank you for helping us with Bog," she says. "Hopefully he won't trouble us again, except when he needs peanut butter and jelly. I'd like to thank you by throwing a party in your honor. But maybe you're tired. If you want, you can have a rest in our library and read some adventure books, then join us later at the party when you're ready."

"What do you want, Sidney?"

"I'm fine either way," he says. "It's up you."

It's time to make a decision. Do you:
Go to the library and read before you go to the party?
P219
Or
Go to the track-keeper party now? **P183**

Finish reading and go to the track-keeper's party

You slide the book back on the shelf. It's time to find out how the track-keeper's party is going. You shake Sidney.

Sidney stretches and yawns. "Are you done reading?"

"Yeah, let's party."

He stands up. "Sounds good to me."

Sharmeena prances through the door. "Ready?"

You nod. "Good timing."

"Great, hop on."

P183

Choose a different lock

It's time to make a decision. Which of the four locks do you want to try this time?

Try the silver lock with blue flashes? **P62**

Try the brass lock engraved with camels? **P64**

Try the green-encrusted lock with dolphins on it? **P68**
Or

Try the plain rusty lock? **P72**

Bend the bars to free Sidney

Bog is still snoring, his warty lips parting to show big teeth when he inhales. As he breathes out, his lips flap like a grandmother's knickers on a washing line. You stifle a snort, until you glimpse another flash of his fangs.

You shudder. "No thanks, I'm not disturbing Bog for the key. He looks way too nasty to tangle with."

You grab the bars of Sidney's cage. A strange tingle goes through your fingers. Weird. You shake your hands and re-grip the bars. There's that tingling sensation again. Ignoring it, you strain with all your might, gritting your teeth and using all your force. The bars start to bend as you force them apart. A soft grunt escapes you.

"Ssh," says Sidney, glancing at Bog, who is stirring in his sleep.

Shaking your hands, you gasp for breath. "Just a little more."

The track-keeper shuffles from hoof to hoof, as if she'd rather be elsewhere.

This time when you grip the bars, your hands start to itch, but you've no time to worry about that, because Bog moans in his sleep and tosses and turns.

"Quick," whispers Sidney.

An enormous fart ruptures from Bog's bottom, and a cloud of purple smelly fog fills the cave. The stench makes your nose itch and eyes water. You stifle a cough and get back to work. Bog could wake up at any moment.

The itching on your hands intensifies, but you ignore it and strain to pull the bars apart until there's a gap wide enough for Sidney to escape.

The moment your drop your hands from the bars, orange fur sprouts from the back of them and spreads along your fingers. Your arms start itching and soon they're furry too. The itch travels over your body, up your neck and face, and down your legs, until you're covered in orange fur. A green beam of light shoots from the middle of your face, shining on Sidney as he clambers out of the cage.

"Wow," he says. "What a great disguise. You look just like our furry track-keeper, here." He gestures at Sharmeena, who is grinning.

Great disguise? Sidney must be joking. This is terrible. You're covered in orange fur, have four legs and only have one eye.

"I told you the bars are enchanted," says Sharmeena. "The only other human that touched them turned into a track-keeper too."

"Not fair. I want to be a track-keeper too," announces Sidney. "Just in case Bog wakes up. There's no way I want to end up as human toast." He rubs his hands up and down the bars until fur starts growing up his arms. It quickly spreads to the rest of the body. Then his head morphs and one giant eye appears in the middle of his face with a grinning mouth underneath. "So cool," he yells.

"No! You'll wake–"

Too late!

With a roar, Bog leaps to his feet. "Where's my toast?" He bellows in a voice that makes the walls of the cave shake.

"Run," calls the Sharmeena, and takes off out the cave door.

With a giant leap, you bound after her with Sidney at your heels.

Your powerful track-keeper legs propel you through the air, yards at a time, like a mountain bike taking a gap jump. This is incredible. Your eye paints the dark tunnel in a green glow, as you chase Sharmeena.

"Amazing," calls Sidney. Then he yelps in pain.

The stench of singed fur fills your nostrils. Behind Sidney, Bog belches fire.

"Come on, Sidney," you yell. "Let's hoof it!"

Sidney gallops up beside you. Together you take off, speeding along the winding tunnel. You belt around a corner and nearly crash into Sharmeena, who is standing staring at the wall. The green beam from her eye is focused, unwavering, on one spot.

"Hurry up," you urge her. "Bog's got flambéed track-keeper on his mind. I don't want to be next on his menu."

Bog's roars make the air pulsate around you.

Sharmeena stands motionless, staring at the wall, as if she's hypnotized. As if she can't hear you. Or Bog.

Sidney tugs at her fur with his mouth, trying to pull her along the tunnel, but she's frozen to the spot.

"Come on," you yell. You can't leave her here for Bog to eat. Not after she helped you.

The glow of Bog's flickering flames dances in the shadows around the corner. He's coming.

"Sidney! What shall we do?" Panic stricken, you turn towards Sidney, but now he's focusing his eye beam on exactly the same spot as Sharmeena. They're both standing still, ignoring the danger.

"Are you two crazy?"

You shoot one last terrified glance backwards. A jet of flame shoots around the corner. Any moment, Bog will be here.

You can't leave Sidney and Sharmeena behind, but you're terrified. Your legs tense to run as one of Bog's giant feet stomps around the corner, making the tunnel floor shake.

"Sidney! Sharmeena!"

Then you notice what they're doing. The beams of green light from Sidney and Sharmeena's eyes are cutting through the rock at the side of the tunnel, like lasers. Maybe they are lasers. Concentrating, you focus your green light on their hole in the rock.

Bog's roars fill your ears. You cringe as a surge of heat blasts along the tunnel, but you stand fast, staring at the rock, your combined laser beams melting a narrow passage through the hard stone.

Bog's flames are getting closer. The heat is nearly unbearable. A spark of pain shoots through your tail. "Ow!" The stink of singed fur hangs in the air.

Gritting your teeth, you send a surge of energy through your eye. Your laser beam blasts through the hole, shattering the last piece of rock standing between you and freedom. Daylight pours through the hole.

"Run!" yells Sharmeena. She shoves you through the hole and leaps in after you.

A moment later, the tunnel behind you is engulfed in flame.

"Quick. To the surface," she yells. "Or he'll burn us alive in this passage."

Your track-keeper legs frantically scramble through the passage. Sidney's breath rasps in your ears. He pushes you forward. Bursting out above ground, you collapse in an exhausted heap, your tail still throbbing where Bog burned it.

Sidney scuttles out behind you and slumps to the ground. Sharmeena climbs out of the tunnel, a lick of flame chasing her. But instead of sprawling on the ground next to you, she kicks dirt down the narrow passage.

Leaping back to your feet, you call to Sidney, "Come on, let's help."

With your strong hind legs, you and Sidney join the track-keeper, kicking dirt until your escape hatch is blocked.

Sharmeena grins. "That should stop Bog for now."

Sidney's pupil whirls with excitement. "Awesome. We filled the hole so fast, it's almost like our hooves are purpose made for digging."

Sharmeena laughs. "They are. We dig all the time. It's part of our job."

Her job? What's she talking about?

"Come on," she says, "I have something to show you. But first, let's get have a drink. That was thirsty work."

You and Sidney reach for your backpacks to grab your bottles, but you don't have arms and you're no longer wearing your backpacks because you're track-keepers. Glancing at each other, you burst out laughing.

"Jase was right, Mystic Portal is a really strange experience," says Sidney.

Grinning at him, you follow the track-keeper through the forest to a stream.

Once you've all slurped up some water, you sit in the stream until your tail is nice and cool again. You climb out onto the bank and shake yourself like a dog.

"Now," says Sharmeena, "you can either become human again and keep riding Mystic Portal on your bikes, or you can stay a while longer and help me build some new jumps."

"So you're the mysterious trail builder?" asks Sidney.

"Yes, it's not just me though. There are many other track-keepers that help."

You smile. "That's generous of you to build trails for us."

"We build them for ourselves. We love doing the jumps and racing each other downhill." Sharmeena laughs. "Of course, we don't mind mountain bikers using them too. Do you want to build a jump or go back to riding?"

Both options sound good. You and Sidney glance at each other.

It's time to make a decision. Do you:

Return to ride Mystic Portal? **P165**

Or

Stay with the track-keeper to build new jumps? **P88**

Stay with the track-keeper to build new jumps

"I don't know about you, Sidney, but I'd love to stay and build some jumps. Digging with these hooves is much easier than with a spade."

"And that's only half of it," says Sharmeena. "Watch this." She taps the back of her heel against the ground. A flat bone-like blade slides out from the front of her leg, just above her hoof.

She leaps into the air and kicks out. The blade slices a chunk out of a log, bark chips spraying into the air. Time and time again, she leaps, lashing out with her hooves at the log.

Soon, the log is curved along the sides and she's formed a diamond pattern on top.

"It's a diamondback snake!" calls Sidney. "That's impressive."

"Wow." The mystery of the track builders has been solved. "So you're the sculptor who has been creating all these cool jumps!"

"Not just me. There's a whole team of us. But this snake is going to take a lot of work to finish. We'll need to build a downhill gap jump over there, and then secure the snake across the top, like a bridge, so bikers can ride along it."

"So you're building a skinny?" you ask.

She nods.

Sidney frowns. "How will the bikes get traction so they don't slip off?"

Sharmeena grins. "The diamond pattern should help the wheels grip. And we can fill the gap with a bed of pine needles in case someone falls."

"Just no pine cones," says Sidney. "I'd rather face Bog than land on a pile of cones." He rubs his bottom, grinning.

She laughs. "Use your bone-blades as spades. They work well for digging too."

You and Sidney tap your heels against the ground. With a strange crunching sensation, blades slide out above your hooves.

"I'll summon more help." Sharmeena lets out a piercing whistle.

Sidney rolls his eyes. "As if that's going to bring an army running."

The ridged bark on a tree trunk in front of you swells and morphs into orange fur, then a track-keeper steps away from the tree.

The green leaves of a bush part, and another track-keeper steps out.

Another emerges from a pile of dirt.

A rock moves, then a green eye appears and orange fur ripples over it.

A track-keeper drops down from a branch. All around you, track-keepers are appearing.

"Usually we camouflage ourselves," says Sharmeena. "Humans can't see us, because we look like dirt, trees or rocks."

"Awesome." Sidney's eyes nearly fall out of his head.

"If you hear a biker coming," says Sharmeena, "hold your breath and you'll instantly be camouflaged. Whatever you're standing next to is what you'll look like."

"Great," you reply, "we'd hate to blow your secret."

Sharmeena grins. "That's the idea. Now let's build that jump."

The track-keepers purr, sounding like a swarm of bees. Some of them fly at the snake, helping to shape it with their blades while others etch diamonds onto its back.

More track-keepers head downhill to start work on the takeoff ramp for the skinny bridge.

You nudge Sidney, who's motionless, staring at them. "Let's get to work." You head down the hill to join the jump builders.

Soon dirt is flying as you, Sidney and the track-keepers churn up earth. Placing a stump on the slope, you sculpt dirt over it. With their teeth, track-keepers drag branches onto the pile until you've built a huge mound, taller than Sidney. Together, you cover it in dirt. Then you and the track-keepers trample all over it, packing it down until it's hard.

When you're finished, you go down the track a few

yards to start work on the bridge's off-ramp. In the middle of building, the crunch of approaching tires sounds further up the track. Instantly, the track-keepers take deep breaths and start merging with the trees, dirt and rocks as their camouflage kicks into action.

"Hold your breath," you hiss to Sidney, and gulp in a mouthful of air. An instant later, Sidney is indistinguishable from the dirt he's standing next to, and you look like a rock.

Tracey yells your name. She skids around a corner, and zooms down the track a few yards from where you're building.

"Sidney," she calls. "Where are you both hiding?"

If only she knew you were in orange fur, camouflaged as a rock!

Her bike zooms past the half-finished jumps, spraying you with loose dirt from your digging. She's frowning, looking really anxious.

A twinge of guilt nags at you. You and Sidney are having the time of your lives, but she looks really worried.

Tracey follows the track around a corner, soon gone from sight.

Around you, track-keepers reappear, emerging from their camouflage.

"Was that your friend?" Sharmeena asks.

"Yeah," answers Sidney. "Maybe we should get back

to her, so she doesn't get too stressed out."

It's time to make a decision. Do you:

Leave the track-keepers and join Tracey? **P148**

Or

Finish building the snake bridge? **P168**

Bypass Ogre Jaws and go down the chicken line

With your spine prickling, you head down the chicken line. It's spooky the way Sidney disappeared in midair. Where has he gone? And what happened to Tracey when she went over Camel Hump? Are you the only one left on the track? Your tires crunch over loose stones and you shoot around a bend, joining up with the main Mystic Portal trail.

Stopping, you place your feet on the ground and take a swig from your water bottle. You glance up and down the trail. No sign of Tracey. Or Sidney. Are they really missing? Or is this just part of the Mystic Portal adventure?

The track in front of you drops away in a steep slope through more forest, thick with undergrowth on each side of the trail. With everyone disappearing, will you ever make it to the beachside exit at the bottom of Mystic Portal?

Tucking your water bottle away, you hop on your pedals and push off.

Thunk! Sidney lands on the trail a few yards in front of you, his tires puffing up a cloud of dust. "Yahoo! Ogre Jaws was awesome!"

"Whoa! Where did you come from?" you yell. It's great that he's here again. Now you don't have to worry. "Seen Tracey?"

"Nah," he calls. "But I bet she's having a *wild* time."
Sidney pedals hard, shooting down the track, zigzagging
between the trees.

You race after him.

Smack! Tracey's bike drops out of nowhere, onto the
track, between you and Sidney.

Freaky.

"Wow, this trail is amazing," she calls, passing Sidney
on a straight. "Let's do the next jump."

You zoom down the track behind Tracey and Sidney,
cornering to take a narrow bridge across a stream. A few
minutes later a switchback heads towards the stream
again and you pass a sign: *Dolphin Slide*.

"Yay, last jump," yells Tracey. "No chicken line!" She
shoots up a huge rock shaped like a dolphin and leaps off
the top, over the stream. In midair, she disappears.

"See you at the beach," calls Sidney as his bike splishes
through a puddle, then zooms up the rock. He jumps and
vanishes.

You gulp. That's right. There's no way out, no chicken
line. The track goes straight ahead and the trees and
bushes are too dense to break through. You head down
the steep slope, through the puddle, your tires hissing
against the rock as you whizz up over Dolphin Slide.

In a flash of blue light, the trail and trees are gone.

You're underwater, riding a dolphin through the
ocean. Sidney and Tracey are riding dolphins too. The

sun slants through the watery blue. A school of purple fish swim past. Below you, a stingray is hiding in the sand. Green seaweed waves in the current, like huge bushy underwater shrubs. A vast bank of colorful coral rises above you like a brightly-colored mosaic. Among the coral, tiny yellow lights wink, casting an eerie glow. What are they? Underwater glow worms?

"Wow," says Tracey. "Can you believe this? It's incredible."

"Hey, we can talk underwater." Bubbles rise from Sidney's mouth as he speaks. "And breathe."

"Amazing. What's next?" you ask. "And how do we get back to Mystic Portal again?"

"I thought you'd never ask," says the dolphin you're riding on.

"Squee," replies Tracey's dolphin, "let's tell them."

Talking dolphins? Wow.

"Welcome to the underwater portion of Mystic Portal," your dolphin says. "My name is Squee, head of this dolphin pod. We're your hosts, today, but you won't just be riding us. In order to get back to Mystic Portal, you need to compete in a race or take a tour. You can choose to ride seahorses in the Round the Coral Peninsula Extravaganza race, or go by turtleback on a Terrific Turtle Tour and see all the underwater sights."

"Cool." Bubbles tickle your nose as you speak. "What do you guys want to do?"

Sidney's eyes are shining. "I'm all for racing. The Round the Coral Peninsula Extravaganza by seahorse is for me."

Tracey's grinning. "I've always wanted to dive, so I'm going on a Terrific Turtle Tour to see all the underwater sights."

"Sounds good," says Squee, swimming under a coral bridge. "What will it be for you?"

It's time to make a decision. Do you:

Ride a seahorse in the Round the Coral Peninsula Extravaganza? **P97**

Or

Ride a turtle on a Terrific Turtle Tour? **P108**

Ride in the Round the Coral Peninsula Extravaganza

You love riding bikes and enjoy racing Sidney whenever you get a chance, but obviously you've never raced on seahorses. It's time to try something new. "Racing seahorses sounds fun."

Sidney's glance slides to you. "I reckon I could beat you," he challenges.

"Oh yeah?" You grin. "Let's see."

You wave as Tracey's dolphin veers towards a group of turtles swimming in and out of some seaweed.

"Turtles look like fun too," Sidney mutters, releasing a trail of bubbles in front of his face. "Maybe we can try those later." His hair floats around his head, like seaweed waving in the current.

Without warning, Squee rolls, tipping you off near a cluster of seahorses. They're huge, big enough for you to sit on, and are all wearing cowboy hats.

"What a laugh." You tap Sidney, who's floating nearby. "Look at their hats."

A blue seahorse wearing a shiny silver sheriff badge swims over to you. He has a belt with holsters holding tiny guns carved of coral. "I beg your pardon?" says the seahorse with a Texan drawl. It has an enormous belly. Could it be pregnant? "I'm Sheriff Kingpin. Did you just laugh at my hat?"

"No, sir, um… ma'am? I was admiring it."

The seahorse stares at you for a few seconds. "Sir to you. Didn't you know that male seahorses carry the mature eggs?" He preens his fins with pride. "I'm the leader of this seahorse ranch. You two will be riding Hippo and Kampos."

A red seahorse sidles over to you, curling his lip as he speaks, "Hippo is my name. Saddle up and climb aboard. It's a shame there are only two of you. Some of our foals and fillies also wanted to race today."

You shoot a nervous glance at Sidney. Hippo seems tough.

"I'm Kampos," a yellow seahorse says to Sidney. "Sheriff Kingpin's carrying my eggs, so I'm racing."

"Um, Hippo," you ask, "why are you named after an enormous mud-wallowing mammal?"

Hippo's lip curls again. "Hippocampus means seahorse."

"And Kampos is ancient Greek for sea monster, so watch it." Kampos laughs, making Hippo smile. Maybe he's not so tough after all.

You ask another question. "You asked me to saddle up, Hippo, but there's no saddle…"

With another of his infamous lip curls, Hippo says brusquely, "Of course there aren't any saddles. We're underwater creatures, not land horses. It was just a saying. Climb aboard and stop mucking around. We want to get this race underway. I've won this race every month and my father and grandfather before me. We have to keep up family tradition." He gives a sly wink and leans towards you, whispering, "Be my rider and we'll win. I know a shortcut. Family secret."

You'll get to take a secret shortcut and beat Sidney. Sounds great.

You and Sidney clamber on the back of Hippo and Kampos.

Sheriff Kingpin addresses you all. "The first event in today's Round the Coral Peninsula Extravaganza is electric eel hurdles. Under no circumstances should you touch a hurdle. If you do…" His face pales.

"What will happen if we touch the eel hurdles?" Sidney pipes up. "Will we get a shock?"

Sheriff Kingpin ignores him, but it can't be good because his face never regains the blue tinge he had when he first swam over.

"Then you'll swim through the treacherous waters of the snapping clams," Kingpin avoids looking at you and Sidney. "Make sure you get through alive. We all know what happened to–"

"Ahem." Hippo clears his throat noisily, then coughs, so you miss most of what Sheriff Kingpin is saying.

"… starting in a few seconds."

Did you miss you something important? Could you die in this race? You nudge Sidney. "What did he say?"

Sidney shrugs. "Don't care, I'm in. This sounds like

fun." At least both of you missed it, so he won't have an advantage in the race.

Two young brown seahorses hold a long piece of seaweed tight in front of you. "Three, two, one, go!" they shout in shrill voices.

Hippo takes off, breaking through the seaweed. You fling your arms around his neck to stop yourself from falling off.

In a flash of yellow, Kampos is swimming alongside Hippo. Sidney whoops. "We're going to beat you," he sings. They race ahead.

"Just try, Sidney," you cry.

"Don't worry. We'll take the shortcut," Hippo whispers.

He surges towards a narrow gap between jagged rocks. Seaweed waves across the entrance, like some bizarre guardian warning you not to pass.

"Are you sure about this?" you ask Hippo.

Clammy seaweed fingers brush across your face and arms as Hippo dives through the rock tunnel with you on his back.

"You'll see," Hippo pants. "This is the fastest route."

The tunnel is so narrow your arms skim jagged outcrops. And so dark, you can only feel and hear Hippo, not see him. You keep your limbs wrapped tight around him. The dark passageway seems to take forever. And this is a shortcut! Hopefully Sidney's route is way longer.

Hippo's panting rasps through the water. He's sounding tired, which doesn't make sense because he told you he always wins. What's wrong?

Ahead, it's growing lighter. A glimpse of blue expands as you near it. You shoot out into the blue ocean, gasping with relief.

"Thankfully we made it," puffs Hippo. "My claustrophobia was kicking in. Sorry about the panting. It always happens when I'm in a tight space."

You laugh in relief. "And I thought you were tired."

"I never get tired." Hippo puffs himself up with pride. "We're nearly there. Remember, whatever you do, don't touch the hurdles."

You round a rocky outcrop. Below you in the pale sand are blue hurdles that flicker with luminous yellow lightning. They're eels with their tails and heads in the sand, and their bodies arched. The hurdle closest to you is a small eel, so it's low, but each gets higher. The last hurdle is a giant eel that towers above the others. How will you ever get over that?

"See, there's Squee." Hippo flicks his tail toward the sleek grey dolphin swimming alongside the hurdles, Sheriff Kingpin beside her. "She's the race marshal."

"Why do we need a marshal when you already have a sheriff?"

"The sheriff protects us against outlaws and leads our ranch. The race marshal makes sure the Extravaganza rules are kept. There are two hurdle rules. First, we must touch the sand between each hurdle. Secondly, we must never–"

"I know. Never touch the hurdles. Will they zap us? Or is their lightning just for show?"

A cry bubbles through the water. It's Sidney, arriving on Kampos.

Ignoring your question, Hippo surges forward, bouncing his tail on the ocean floor. A puff of sand rises around you as he leaps the first hurdle.

Your head-start is tiny, but hopefully it will last.

With another bounce in the sand, Hippo flies over the second hurdle. This is fun. The third hurdle is a little higher. You feel Hippo strain, but he easily clears it.

As Hippo bounces up towards a fourth hurdle, Kampos lands below you, stirring up the sand on the ocean floor.

They're gaining! "Come on, Hippo," you cry.

Sidney and Kampos clear the next hurdle and touch down beside you on the ocean floor. Kampos and Hippo are neck and neck as they jump over the next hurdle. Everything becomes a blur of sand and hurdles as you and Hippo grunt, straining to keep up with Sidney and Kampos.

Landing on the sand, the final hurdle looms above you. In a blurry yellow streak, Sidney and Kampos zoom over it and race off.

"I can't do it," pants Hippo. "I've been too lazy, not training because I always win, but Kampos has been practicing every day. I might not clear the final hurdle. We could end up touching it."

"And what will happen then?" You ask.

"You don't want to know. But it's horrible." His red face pales to pink.

"So we're giving up?"

"It's your choice," Hippo says. "We could still catch up on the snapping clams. There's always a chance that they'll run into problems, so we could still win and honor my forefathers."

"I have an idea!" you exclaim. "I can help you over this hurdle by kicking as we leap upwards. That should help us clear it."

"We can try if you want," says Hippo. "I still think it's too risky, but it's your race, so it's your choice."

Sheriff Kingpin is floating nearby. He stares at the hurdle, shaking his head, his expression grim.

"Be careful what you choose," warns Squee.

It's time to make a decision. Do you:

Kick to help Hippo over the last hurdle? **P104**

Or

Go to the snapping clams? **P106**

Kick to help Hippo over the last hurdle

What could be so dangerous about touching a hurdle? Maybe these seahorses are really chickens, too scared to try. Or perhaps they're superstitious. Besides, you're not planning on touching the hurdle. Your legs are strong from mountain biking. Their added strength should make a difference and help Hippo clear the flickering hurdle towering above you.

"Come on, Hippo." You pat his back. "Let's leap this hurdle and catch up to Sidney and Kampos."

Hippo starts trembling. "S-sure," he stutters.

He seems really scared. Have you made the right choice?

It's time to make a decision. Do you:

Abandon the highest hurdle and go to the snapping clams? **P106**

Or

Leap the final hurdle? **P120**

Abandon the hurdle and go to the snapping clams

You hate to see Hippo so frightened. "Sorry, Hippo I didn't mean to scare you." You pat his trembling body. "Let's just go to the snapping clams and try to catch up to Sidney and Kampos."

Hippo stops trembling. "I'm so glad," he says, swimming away from the hurdles.

Sheriff Kingpin cheers. "Great choice."

You've made a good choice. Turn the page to go to the snapping clams. **P106**

The snapping clams

"Snapping clams sound dangerous too," you say, "but I'm going to take your advice. You know these waters better than me."

"Good idea," calls Sheriff Kingpin.

Squee nods her head in agreement.

With a flip of his tail, Hippo zooms under the hurdle, and out over the sand. "I'm glad we didn't touch that hurdle or we really would've suffered."

"How?"

"Brrr. I don't want to discuss it. It's too awful."

"Come on. What?"

"Can't tell, but let me say, you're in the ocean," says Hippo, "not on some tame mountain biking trail."

Mystic Portal is far from tame, but you don't argue. You're just glad you didn't crash into one of the squid's hurdles. What's ahead of you, now? Snapping clams don't sound very tame either.

Skirting a large bank of seaweed, you come to a series of rocks with giant clams perched on top of them. The clams are opening and shutting their shells.

As Hippo approaches the clams, Sidney and Kampos swim out from the third clam, racing towards the fourth.

"Eight snapping clams in all," says Hippo.

"What are the rules?"

Hippo rolls his eyes. "Pretty obvious. Don't get

snapped." With that, he zooms forward, his body nearly parallel with the ocean floor.

The first giant clam looms in front of you, its shell wide open, exposing its fleshy interior. That's strange, you thought clam meat was white or creamy, but this clam has bluish-yellow flesh. Perhaps it's the underwater light that makes it look that way.

Before you have more time to think, you're out the other side, shooting towards the second clam. This one has its wide jaws half open. It stretches them further as you pass through. In the middle of its flesh, something shiny winks at you. "Is that a pearl?"

"Of course." Hippo shoots out of the clam leaving the pearl behind.

It's the size of a baseball. With a pearl like that, you could buy a new mountain bike. Maybe even one for Sidney too. "Is there any chance of me grabbing a pearl?"

"Don't even think about it," snaps Hippo. "It's way too dangerous."

When Hippo enters the next clam, a giant pearl is lying on the flesh. If you jump off Hippo's back, just for a second, you could grab it.

It's time to make a decision. Do you:

Leap off Hippo's back and grab the pearl? **P137**

Or

Stay on Hippo's back and go to the next clam? **P139**

Ride a turtle on a Terrific Turtle Tour

Cruising by turtleback sounds much more relaxing than racing on a seahorse.

"I'm coming too, Tracey." You grin. "I'd love a tour on turtleback."

"I wonder what we're going to see." Tracey's eyes are alight with excitement.

Squee and Tracey's dolphin swim over to a group of turtles playing leapfrog in some seaweed. Golden flowers glint among the seaweed. It's hard to tell how many turtles there are, because the brown and green seaweed camouflages their shells so well.

Squee whistles.

Three giant turtles break away from the group and swim towards you. One of them has a piece of seaweed wrapped around its leg.

"I'm Tuck," says the largest in a deep voice.

"And I'm Nip," says one with a ragged edge on its shell.

The turtle with seaweed around its leg bobs up and down in the water. "And I'm tagging along to learn how to be a tour guide. I've never done this before and I'm really excited. I'm especially looking forward to—"

"Ssh!" Nip whispers. "That's enough, just tell them your name, Junior."

"I'm Junior." The turtle pipes up, beaming.

Junior doesn't look any smaller than the others, but his voice is squeaky, like a child's.

"Pleased to meet you," you reply. "Do you mind telling me what that seaweed is for?" You point to the seaweed around his leg.

"Sure, that's my leash." Junior puffs up his chest. "When I'm a proper tour guide, I won't have to use it."

"Thanks for offering to take us on a Terrific Turtle Tour," says Tracey in her best polite voice, the one she uses with adults. "What would you like to show us?"

"A Terrific Turtle Tour?" says Junior before the others can get a word in. "Here's a tour of a terrific turtle. Well, here's my shell. These are my forelegs and these are my hind legs. He spins in the water. "And this is my tail." He lifts it and a stream of bubbles drifts out from the back end of his shell. His face goes bright red. "Um, sorry," he mutters.

"Junior!" Nip reprimands, tugging his leash.

"Um, time to swim over here," says Tuck, but not before an unpleasant odor drifts on the current towards you.

Tracey splutters and leaps off her dolphin to swim after Tuck. She clambers aboard his shell.

Squee whistles goodbye and you swim after them, leaving the smelly water behind.

Nip nods her head. "Climb aboard."

You glance at Junior.

"Sorry," he says, "I had too many kelp cakes for breakfast. By the way, I can't carry you because I'm too inexperienced to carry passengers. Soon I'll be qualified with my passenger license then I'll–"

"Ssh!" Tuck tugs his leash. "That's enough. Get on with the tour introductions."

"Oh, yes." Junior nibbles his lip.

He reminds you of Tracey when she's trying to come up with a quick excuse for not doing her homework or Sidney when he's trying to explain to his mom why his pants are ripped – again.

Junior speaks slowly, concentrating. "Today you can choose between the Sunken Ship Tour and the Underwater City Tour."

"Go on," says Nip. "Say the rest."

"But you're always telling me to say less," says Junior.

"Junior!" snaps Tuck.

Junior winks, without his parents seeing. You get the feeling he's used to stringing them along like this. "Our sunken ship tour–"

"Junior," interrupts Nip. "Sunken Ship Tour has capitals."

Junior rolls his eyes and puts on a voice like a TV news anchor. "Our Sunken Ship Tour has a variety of interesting aspects. The *Pyromania*, an ancient pirate galleon, has been on our ocean floor for years, giving the ocean's flora and fauna a chance to flourish in new habitats within this man-made structure. Of particular interest is the shark hatchery." Junior's voice changes and he sounds like himself again. "Oh, the ship's fun, and really, really exciting. You should see it."

"What about the underwater city?" asks Tracey. "That sounds interesting too."

Junior puts on his TV voice again. "The underwater city of Hydropolis was flooded approximately twenty years ago when sea levels rose. Fortunately, the people of Hydropolis fled and survived. The city, however, was not so fortunate, and was flooded overnight. The waterlogged landmass slowly subsided into the sea over two years, creating a fantastic tourist attraction for Terrific Turtle Tours. Should you choose the Hydropolis Underwater City Tour, you're guaranteed a thrilling adventure of adrenaline rushes."

Junior grins, then continues, "Of course the *Pyromania* Sunken Ship Tour is also a veritable wonderland of undersea treasures – a murky pirate world full of intrigue and mystery."

Tuck clears his throat. "So, which will it be? The Hydropolis Underwater City Tour? Or the *Pyromania* Sunken Ship Tour?

Straddled across Tuck's shell, Tracey shrugs. "Both sound exciting. It's up to you."

You scratch your head as you think about what to do.

It's time to make a decision. Which Terrific Turtle

Tour would you like to go on?

The Hydropolis Underwater City Tour? **P157**

Or

The *Pyromania* Sunken Ship Tour? **P113**

The *Pyromania* Sunken Ship Tour

"I've always wanted to see a pirate ship. Could we go on the *Pyromania* tour?"

"What does *Pyromania* mean?" asks Tracey.

"Not sure," says Junior. "Maybe it means you're mad about being a pirate. You know, Pyro for pirate and mania…"

"Ahem," coughs Tuck. "*Pyromania* means crazy pirates. Everyone knows that."

You smother a chuckle. Your teacher taught you that a pyromaniac is someone who likes lighting fires. What a weird name for a pirate ship.

"Let's get going," says Nip, "before the next tourists get here for a tour."

You cling to her shell as she swims into deeper water.

Fish cruise the ocean searching for tasty treats – blue fish with yellow fins, red ones, and others with purple and orange stripes. A shoal of tiny silver fish flit past. Starfish laze around on rocks, like sunbathers. A stingray moves along the ocean floor, churning up clouds of sand.

A dark shape looms on the ocean floor. As you get closer, the shipwreck comes into view. The *Pyromania* is leaning to one side. Colorful seaweed adorns the mast. The wood of the hull is nearly black, aged from years under the sea.

"Is there any pirate treasure?" asks Tracey.

"Treasure?" says Junior. "No. Dad thought treasure hunters would've been bad for Terrific Turtle Tours' business, so he got rid of the treasure long ago."

Tracey rolls her eyes and leans over towards you, so the turtles can't hear. "I bet they threw it away," she whispers. "What a waste."

You feel the same. You could have bought new bikes for everyone with a single gold doubloon. Turtles probably have no idea how valuable treasure is.

Nip and Tuck settle on the railing of the ship. "Junior, we're a little tired, so we'll rest here. You've done this tour often enough, so today you can guide our adventurers. Be careful and remember everything we've taught you."

Junior guides you and Tracey through the hatchway. Below deck, loose planks are strewn around the floor.

"Treasure seekers did that." Junior shakes his head. "Imagine ripping planks off a perfectly good wreck. It's such terrible vandalism!"

Vandalism? You never would have thought that hunting for treasure could be vandalism. But it obviously is in the eyes of these sea creatures.

You come to a door. "What's behind that?"

"My parents tell me never to let people open that door." Junior winks. "But they're not around, so maybe we can have a look."

"Why?" you ask. "What's in there?"

"It's a shark hatchery," says Junior. "But they're only tiny, so they'll be harmless."

"Wow, I've always wanted to swim with baby sharks," says Tracey. "Go on, please open it."

You glance at Tracey. She shrugs, and tugs the rusty metal handle. "It's stiff. I'm going to need your help."

You grab the handle and heave. The door flies open and a swarm of silver baby sharks shoot past you.

"They're cute," Tracey croons. "No one would ever believe they could grow up to be killers."

You peer inside the hatchery, but it's too gloomy to see much. "I can't see any more babies. Is it a problem that we let them out?"

Before anyone can answer, a sleek white and grey form fills the doorway and opens its massive jaws. A wall of jagged teeth fills your vision.

"No," screams Junior, diving between you and the shark.

The shark's mouth snaps shut. Junior squirms and writhes, but his shell is caught between the shark's teeth. "Swim!" He cries. "Swim away, fast!" Then his eyes close and he goes limp in the shark's jaws.

It's time to make a decision. Do you:

Flee from the shark with Tracey? **P135**

Or

Save Junior from the shark? **P150**

Stay in the tunnel

Sidney's a good friend, but you have no idea how to fight an ogre and you're not keen to learn. "I'm not going with you," you state firmly, staring into Sharmeena's eye. "Besides, I don't know how to fight ogres so I'd probably get in your way."

"You're too scared." She pokes out her tongue. "Anyone who abandons their friend to Bog is no friend of mine."

With a flash of fur, bathed in the eerie light from her eye, the track-keeper leaps over you, and disappears around a corner.

You gulp. It's darker here than inside a trouser pocket.

No point in staying here. If you follow Sharmeena, at least you'll be able to see something. Feeling your way along the tunnel walls, you round the corner. Wow, that track-keeper moves fast. The glow of her eye is a pinprick, miles down the tunnel.

You can hardly see a thing. Hands out, you run your fingers along the tunnel wall, over roots and crumbling dirt, and inch your way forward. Soon the track-keeper's green light is gone.

But what's that?

Something yellow and glowing is coming towards you. It's a naked flame. It could be someone carrying an old-fashioned torch.

"Hey," you call. "Over here."

An ominous roar ripples down the tunnel towards you, making the ground tremble.

Uh-oh. That doesn't sound like good news. Spinning, you race back the way you came, stumbling over tree roots and skinning your knees. Scrambling to your feet, a blast of heat radiates down the tunnel towards you.

You whirl.

And face an ogre belching fire, its teeth glinting among the flames.

No wonder he can toast kids, Bog the ogre breathes fire. Your knees shake so hard, you can't move.

Bog approaches. The stench of swamp wafts towards you. That must be how he got his name.

"My toast ran away," Bog roars. "Need another toast. Don't worry, I gobble you fast. Too fast for pain."

Although you struggle to move your feet, you're paralyzed, too scared to move.

Bog roars, belching flame. "Caught you!"

Sorry, this part of your story is over. You've taken a great jump, met a cool creature and had a wild adventure, but abandoning Sidney to Bog was not the best choice you could've made. There are still many other adventures. You could ride a camel, fight desert bandits, meet dolphins or build a new bike jump with Sidney and the mysterious track builders of Mystic Portal.

It's time to make a decision. Do you:

Go back and help Sharmeena save Sidney from Bog?
P53

Go to the list of choices and start reading from another part of the story? **P248**

Or

Go back to the beginning a try another path? **P1**

Go ahead despite the sparks

You were warned about playing with electricity when you were child, but you're desperate. You have to save Sidney.

"I'm fine. I've got this."

"I wouldn't, if I were you," Sharmeena cautions.

You jam the key into the lock. A jolt flies down your arms and your whole body shudders. Your heart spasms painfully, then everything goes black.

Sorry, this part of your story is over. The lock gave you an electrical shock, killing you instantly. Taking a chance on a lock charged with an electrical force field was not the best choice, so you didn't save Sidney from Bog. But you can choose again. You could become a camel racer, have an underwater adventure on a sea turtle, or tame Bog the ogre.

It's time to make a decision. You have 3 choices. Do you:

Choose a different lock? **P80**

Go to the list of choices and start reading from another part of the story? **P248**

Or

Go back to the beginning a try another path? **P1**

Leap the final hurdle

"Come on, Hippo," you say, "have courage."

"Alright." Some of his earlier bravado sneaks back into his voice. "Let's do this. On the count of three. One, two, three."

He jumps up from the sand, then lands again and bounces, swimming up towards the hurdle. "Kick, now."

Releasing your grip around his stomach, you fling your feet backwards and kick like crazy. It's working. You're rising upwards towards the top of the hurdle. The eel's skin flickers with luminous yellow electricity. You keep kicking, churning up bubbles as you rise through the water.

The hurdle is nearly in reach, when Hippo starts to falter. "I c-can't do it,'" he pants.

"Yes we can," you yell. "Don't give up."

Within a huge kick, you both surge above the hurdle. "We're over!" you yell, bubbles flying around your face. "We've done it."

"No we haven't," shrieks Hippo. "My tail's stuck."

He's right. The curly end of his tail is hooked under the top of the hurdle. Yellow sparks flit around his trapped tail.

"No problem. I'll just swim down and free it."

"No," shrieks Hippo. "Swim away while you can. Hurry."

The lightning from the electric eels must be dangerous, but it's your fault Hippo's stuck. You leap off his back and open your backpack. "Hold on I'll get my bike's spare inner tube. Rubber is a great insulator, so this won't hurt either of us." Fishing out a tire tube, you hook it around Hippo and yank him off the hurdle. The yellow lightning running across the eels bodies dims.

"Are you okay?" you ask.

He nods. "Sure, I'm fine." But his tail has lost its cute curl and hangs limp in the sea. "Brace yourself."

"For what?"

The electric eels' lightning goes out. The lights on all those underwater glow worms die. The sea is darker than inside a sunken treasure chest.

"Blistering barnacles and crusty coral, now we've done it!" Hippo curses.

"What? Where are you, Hippo? I can't see a thing. And where are Kampos and Sidney?"

"We've deactivated the grid," answers Hippo.

"What grid?"

Before he can answer, beams of light shoot through the dark and a school of anglerfish surround you. The lights hanging off their heads illuminate the area.

"Fins up, you're under arrest for deactivating the power grid."

You don't have fins, so you raise your hands.

Hippo's fins poke straight up.

"As members of the Municipal Eel Charmers, we hereby arrest you and recruit you to eel charming, until all the eels that power this area have been persuaded to resume their duties in the power grid."

That's when you realize the electric eels are nowhere to be seen.

The angler fish pass you flutes made of coral. "Using the eel's power grid as hurdles is fine, as long as you don't tamper with the power. But now, as a result of your clumsiness, you must patrol the Coral Peninsula and charm the eels out of their hideouts, so Seahorse Ranch has light again. You will be assigned two guards who will report back to us when the eels are in place."

Two angler fish with gaping sharp-toothed smiles flank you as you ride off with Hippo. But when you play the pipe, an awful screech comes out, making you wince.

"Agh! I hate that noise," Hippos snaps. "But the electric eels love it."

An eel pokes its head out of the coral and follows you.

"This is like snake charming," you mutter, as the eel weaves through the seaweed towards you.

"What's that?" asks Hippo.

"Um, don't worry." You play another squeaky tune. It's horrible, off key and discordant. The music grates against your teeth.

By late afternoon, you've summoned all the eels from their nooks and crannies with your bad melodies. Your ears ache. You never want to play another coral pipe in your life.

It takes another hour of Hippo's smooth talking to convince the electric eels to take their positions back in the grid. When they're all lined up in their hurdle spots again, tiny lights among the coral flicker on again. The area is bathed in light.

"Don't touch the hurdles again," warn the anglerfish before they leave.

You nudge Hippo. "Those aren't undersea glow worms. They're lights."

Hippo winks at you. "Want to jump the eel hurdles again?"

"No thanks, I don't fancy playing more tunes on that pipe. My ears are still ringing from the last lot."

"Mine too."

His lip curls as Sidney and Kampos appear. "Where have you two been? You missed all the action."

"It was so dark," says Sidney. "We couldn't see a thing until a minute ago, so we had to sit tight."

"You tripped the grid, didn't you?" asks Kampos.

You and Hippo grin. "Yeah, we've been charming eels," you reply.

"Rather you than us," Kampos says.

Sheriff Kingpin appears, rubbing his huge belly. "Power outage, huh? Glad to see you fixed it, but it's time for you to go home now. The race is over."

Kampos and Hippo swim under a coral arch.

"Farewell," they call.

"Bye."

Moments later, you and Sidney are riding along Mystic Portal on your bikes. "I'm changing to my granny gear," calls Sidney as you head up a hill.

He's forgotten you don't have gears. You groan, but as you ride up the slope, your pedals crackle and small bolts of lightning fly from them. Humming, your bike zooms up the hill.

"Hey," calls Sidney, "our bikes are powered with electricity. How did that happen?"

Tracey is parked at the top of the hill. "You guys are motoring," she calls. "Tell me your secret."

"Haven't got one," yells Sidney.

That's when you spy the engraving of an electric eel on your handlebars.

Congratulations, this part of your adventure is over, even if your ears are still ringing from those awful tunes. You rode a seahorse, sorted out the eel's power grid and had fun on your mountain bike. You could go back and see what happens if you choose not to jump the final hurdle, but there are also many other adventures on Mystic Portal. You could tame an ogre, ride a magic carpet, learn how to survive in the desert, or help build a mountain bike jump.

It's time to make a decision. Do you:

Go to the snapping clams? **P106**

Go to the list of choices and start reading from another part of the story? **P248**

Or

Go back to the beginning a try another path? **P1**

Leave the oasis

"Excuse me, Aamir, I don't mean any offence, but I have a family too, and need to return to them."

"Very well." He nods, but doesn't look happy at all. "The law of the desert states that every visitor to our oasis is welcome to water from the lake and fruit from the trees. I cannot spare a camel to transport you. The nearest town is a day's walk in that direction." He points beyond the lake. "Straight ahead. Good luck."

Next to him, Latifah looks worried.

You gaze out over the burning red sand and gulp. A whole day's walk? "Um, maybe I will race your camel."

Aamir scowls. "I'm sorry. Racing a camel is a great honor. You turned me down." As Aamir turns his back on you, Latifah passes you a water skin, and a small pouch containing oranges and dates.

Jamina nuzzles your hand. "Good luck," she says. "Remember the desert survival lessons I taught you."

There's nothing for it, you have to face the desert alone. Squaring your shoulders, you nod farewell to Jamina and Latifah, and start walking over the hot sand. Heading over an enormous dune, your feet flounder but you reach the top. Soon the oasis is out of sight.

You can do this, you know you can. As long as you head in the right direction, you should reach the city. Determined to make good time, you race down the dune, keeping an eye on the sun to make sure you're heading in the right direction.

The sun beats down mercilessly, hour after hour. You drink deeply from your bottle until it's empty, munching on oranges and figs to keep your strength up. Your feet drag in the sand. Your eyes are dry and gritty. It's important to stay hydrated, so you open the water skin and have a drink from that too.

Sweat beads your face, running into your eyes, stinging them. As you stumble up yet another dune an ominous buzz sounds on the other side.

Dropping to your belly, you crawl commando style to the top to take a look. Flies are buzzing around an animal's carcass as vultures tear strips off it. You wrinkle your nose – even from here it stinks. Oh well, the city lies on the other side of that carcass so, as exhausted as you are, and as much as it smells, you'll have to pass it.

You take another deep swig from the water skin, only to realize it's now empty. Alarm bells ring in your head. How silly could you be? Jamina taught you to only take small sips of water, but in your desperation to get to the city, you've finished all your water in a few hours. And you only have one orange left.

Sliding down the dune towards the carcass, you hope there'll be another oasis on the way so you can refill the water skin. Not wanting to disturb the vultures, you make a wide berth around the carcass. But as you pass, a cloud of flies rise into the air and zoom towards you. You scramble across sand.

The flies are faster. They swarm onto your face.

Hands thrashing, you try to swat them away, but the minute you succeed, more land on your forehead, cheeks and neck. It's a losing battle. They're drinking your sweat – here in the desert every drop of fluid is precious. Perhaps that was one of the reasons Jamina said to sip water – to prevent sweat. You continue walking, flies crawling over your face.

If only you had a wide-brimmed Australian hat with corks dangling around it. That would keep the flies off. Hey, you don't have a hat, but you do have a sweatshirt. Pulling it out of your backpack, you tie it around your head, covering most of your face so the flies can't land.

Hours later, you come over a dune and see footprints in the sand. Parched and dizzy from lack of water, you follow them, hoping to catch up with someone who can give you a drink. Soon you're shuffling through the sand, exhausted, when you notice there are two sets of footprints. Two people? You press ahead, ignoring your throbbing skull and dry throat.

Now there are three sets of footprints.

With horror, you realize you've been walking in circles, following yourself. You stare at the sun, trying to orient yourself, but no longer know which way the city lies. Or the oasis.

Striking out into the hot red sand, you press forward. Soon you're crawling up a huge dune that seems to go on forever. Your hands and knees sink into the soft sand, but you drag yourself upwards until you crest the hill. Below is a tiny oasis. At the foot of a lone palm is a pool of sparkling cool water.

"Yahoo." Your voice only comes out as a croak. Giving into exhaustion, you roll down the dune, and then crawl across the sand to the oasis. Scooping up cool water with your hands, you bring it to your mouth, drinking greedily.

And end up with a mouthful of sand.

"Gah!"

It was a mirage – a hallucination from being dehydrated and exhausted. There was no oasis. It was all your imagination. You're never going to get to the city. Exhausted, you sink to the sand. If only you'd stayed for the camel races.

Sorry, this part of your adventure is over. You die in the desert. Turning down camel racing was not the best idea, especially when Aamir warned you to accept. You and Tracey never re-appear from Mystic Portal. For the rest of their lives, Sidney and your families wonder what happened. But don't worry, there are lots of other adventures in Mystic Portal, so you can choose again. Maybe you'd like to race Jamina, meet an ogre, explore the underwater city of Hydropolis or build a mountain bike jump.

It's time to make a decision. Do you:

Go back and race Jamina in the Camel races? **P206**

Go to the list of choices and start reading from another part of the story? **P248**

Or

Go back to the beginning a try another path? **P1**

Keep Jamina running from the sandstorm

"We can make it, I'm sure we can. Keep running."

Jamina increases speed, jolting you even more. Hanging onto the saddle with one hand, you tug your sweatshirt tighter around your face to keep the stinging grains away from your skin.

Red dust thickens the air, making you choke and cough. Squeezing your eyes shut against blasts of sand, you hang on to Jamina. She dashes forward, lurching and stumbling, nearly pitching you from the saddle.

Clutching the reins tightly, you catch your balance, but the camel's lurching gait nearly knocks you off again. For ages, you hang on, eyes shut tight, as she bucks like a bronco trying to make headway against the vicious storm.

"Mwoooaaaah!" Jamina shrieks.

You're jolted from the saddle, flying through the cloud of red. "Oof." Sand is harder than you thought, but luckily none of your bones are broken. You attempt to scramble to your feet, but the wind knocks you down.

Through the surging red sand, you hear Jamina bellow. You crawl towards her. Despite the raging sandstorm, you soon butt against something warm and solid.

"Jamina. Are you okay?"

"I was worried I'd lost you."

"I'll try to pitch the tent." You feel your way along her saddle, the sand pelting your fumbling fingers. But as you loosen the tent, the wind catches it and hurls it out of your grasp. You squint through the red haze, but it's already lost from view.

"Burrow into my side," says Jamina.

The wind dies down.

"Welcome to Sands of Time Industries," someone says.

You raise your head. The sandstorm is gone. You're in a warehouse – no wait, it's the biggest tent you could ever imagine. At one end, there's something that looks like a pizza oven, where people are working with long thin pipes.

As you watch, a female factory worker blows into the pipes and a bubble starts forming. That's right, glass is made from sand. That woman is glassblowing. The object on the end of the pipe is forming a familiar shape, like a three-dimensional figure of eight.

It's an hour glass.

"You'll start here," says a woman beside you, tugging your shirt. She's pointing to a table where three other kids, also dressed in mountain bike gear, are putting sand into hour glasses.

"Went down Camel Hump, did you?" asks one of the workers at the table.

"Didn't pitch the tent?" asks another.

You nod, stunned. One second you were drowning in sand and now...

"Well, you only have to work for one hour before you get to go home," says the first worker. He looks like Jase, a fellow-mountain biker, but older. Perhaps he's Jase's big brother.

"Do you know Jase?" you ask.

He frowns at you, puzzled. "What do you mean, 'Do I know Jase?' I am Jase!" He grins. "Welcome to Sands of Time. Just fill this hour glass and you can go home. The good news is, like I said, it'll only take an hour." He passes you an hour glass.

"Th-thanks." You gulp. Jase has aged. He looks years older – but you and Sidney only went riding with him a week ago.

You pick up a few grains of sand and drop them into the open end of the hour glass. One grain trickles slowly into the neck of the glass. The others float out the top, back onto the pile.

"Just a grain at a time, no more is allowed," a girl next to you says.

Crazy. This'll take forever.

"Hey, I used to know you. A shame you didn't pitch the tent. You could've been home by now." She looks like an older version of Tracey.

Grinning, Jase says, "It's only an hour, but there's bad news too. Time goes a lot more slowly here, but our aging process doesn't slow, so we become wrinkled and old in no time at all."

Your spine prickles as you pick up your next grain of sand.

Sorry, this part of your adventure is over. Running away from sandstorms is usually fatal, so you were lucky to be saved by Sands of Time Industries. Pitching a tent against the storm would've been a much better strategy, because you, Tracey, Jase and the other workers spend the rest of your lives each trying to fill an hour glass. Sidney waited for ages at the bottom of Mystic Portal, but never saw you or Tracey again. The only thing he could tell your families was that you both disappeared in midair. There are lots of other adventures in Mystic Portal, because you can choose again. Maybe you'll ride the magic carpet with Tracey, tame an ogre or turn into a furry creature. You may even get to visit a sunken pirate ship.

It's time to make a decision. You have 3 choices. Do you:

Go back and pitch the tent? **P15**

Go to the list of choices and start reading from another part of the story? **P248**

Or

Go back to the beginning a try another path? **P1**

Flee from the shark with Tracey

"We have to save him," Tracey screams.

"It's too late. He's dead. We have to save ourselves."

Grabbing Tracey's arm, you tug her away from the shark, which is now shaking Junior from side to side in its jaws.

You and Tracey swim towards a porthole and scramble through. The shark will never fit through, so you should be safe.

Tracey's voice shakes. "Wow, am I glad we escaped that—" Then her mouth opens in an underwater scream.

You spin to face two great white sharks, twice as large as the one you just fled from. Their jaws open and they lunge at you. There's no escape. You're fish food. This is your fin-ale.

Sorry, this part of your story is over. Abandoning Junior in his time of need (when he tried to save you) was not the best decision.

But don't worry, you can choose again. Maybe you'd like to go back and save Junior, explore the underwater city of Hydropolis, or ride a seahorse in the Round the Coral Peninsula Extravaganza.

Or perhaps you'd like to do another jump on Mystic Portal.

It's time to make a decision. Do you:

Go back and save Junior? **P150**

Go to the list of choices and start reading from another part of the story? **P248**

Or

Go back to the beginning a try another path? **P1**

Leap off Hippo's back and grab the pearl

Without thinking, you dive off Hippo's back, landing in the clam's soft flesh. The clam quivers as you walk towards the pearl.

Hippo charges out of the clam, then spins to face you. "No. Don't touch that pearl. It's not yours to take." His voice is panicky. "Get out of there, quick."

The pearl glints at you, full of promise. This pearl could give you new mountain bike – a bike with full suspension, just like Tracey's. It'll be like landing on a feather duvet every time you make a jump.

"I'm fine," you yell, stepping towards the pearl. The clam's flesh quivers again, more violently. It grows darker. Swiveling, you realize the jaws of the clam are closing.

You lunge, diving across the clam. Gripping the enormous pearl with both hands, you tug it.

It holds fast.

You can't let go. This pearl represents your dreams, your new bike. You yank hard, and the pearl comes free in your hands.

The clam snaps shut and you're enveloped in darkness. You sit down, the pearl in your arms, and wait for the clam to open.

You wait.

And wait.

Your chest grows tight. There's less and less oxygen in the water inside the clam.

Outside, someone knocks on the shell. Voices yell. They're trying to get you out.

But it's too late. Your breathing becomes shallow. Suddenly, like a flat tire, you're out of air.

Sorry, this part of your adventure is over. Your guide, Hippo, told you that the pearl was not yours to take. Ignoring his advice was not the wisest decision. Never mind, you can go back and make another choice. There are plenty of other adventures on Mystic Portal, so do choose again.

It's time to make a decision. You have 3 choices. Do you:

Stay on Hippo's back and go to the next clam? **P139**

Go to the list of choices and start reading from another part of the story? **P248**

Or

Go back to the beginning a try another path? **P1**

Stay on Hippo's back and go to the next clam

Although you could buy a new bike with this pearl, Hippo said it would be dangerous to take it. He also mentioned that it wasn't yours to take.

With one last backward glance, you cling tightly to his back as he churns through the water, out the other side of the clam.

The clam shell snaps shut behind you. You shudder. If you'd delayed to get the pearl, you may have had a limb snapped off in that shell, or even worse, been trapped inside.

You zoom through two more clams, glad you're not trapped.

"Am I imagining it, or are these clams shutting their shells faster than the others?"

Hippo laughs. "That's part of the fun. These ones are much faster. That's why they're called snapping clams."

He picks up speed, rocketing towards a closed shell. Just when you think you're going to hit the hard grey exterior of the clam, it opens. Hippo zooms through the middle. The clam clicks shut behind him.

"Close call." A voice drifts on the current.

Startled, you glance around. It doesn't sound like Sidney.

There, to your left, swimming above the wreckage of an old ship, are a two turtles with kids riding on their backs.

"Just ignore those turtle tours," says Hippo, snorting. "Those tourists have nothing better to do than stare."

He's right. They're just hanging around in the water watching you race. You grin, glad you're having fun, and zip through the next clam.

Only two more clams to go.

When you clear the next clam, you give the tourists the thumbs up sign.

They're looking worried, but they've nothing to be afraid of. It's you who's taking the risks, not them.

The last clam is right in front of you.

"Hold on tight, and stay flat against my back," urges Hippo as you whizz through the clam.

Leaning low, you keep your head down. Ahead, the clam shell is shutting – there are only seconds to get out.

Now, it's only open a crack.

Hippo makes the gap. You sit up, waving your arms in victory.

The next moment, you're yanked off Hippo's back. You pull and tug, but you can't move. Glancing over your shoulder, you realize the end of your backpack straps are trapped in the clam shell.

Hippo speeds away, without you.

"Hippo!"

He doesn't seem to hear you.

You try to struggle out of your backpack, but as you

tug, the straps only get tighter, held fast by the clam. Your shoulders ache from yanking against the clam's grip. You're stuck.

Something touches your arm, making you flinch. Is it the clam? You turn your head. "Oh, hi."

"Need a hand?" On turtle back, a kid is holding up a knife. "I can cut the ends of your straps off, and get you out."

"That'd be great."

The kid balances on the edge of the turtle's back, leaning with one arm on the clam's shell, and saws at your backpack straps.

You tumble through the water, landing on the sand. The ends of your straps are hanging from the clam's shell.

"Thank you." You grin, flexing your shoulders. "You saved my life, and my straps were too long anyway."

"No problem, I'll see you around Mystic Portal." The turtle swims away and the kid rejoins the tour.

A familiar voice sounds behind you. "An excellent solution, even if it was from a turtle rider."

You whirl. "Hippo! I thought you'd gone."

"By the time I realized I'd lost you, that turtle rider was already helping. Climb aboard, we have to get to the finish line."

"But we've lost the race already."

"No we haven't." Hippo's lip curls. "There are no

losers in this race, except those that don't finish. Although the first home is the winner."

You hold on tight as Hippo races over coral bridges, through gardens of purple and yellow anemones, and waving forests of green seaweed. He swims past a wall of coral, twisted in beautiful multi-colored formations.

"When I was a young seahorse, I played a game with my brothers and sisters, imagining what these coral sculptures were."

"I see what you mean. That one looks like a goblin." You point at a green formation with appendages like arms and legs and a gaping hole that could be a mouth.

"This one looks like a seahorse's belly, full of eggs," says Hippo, nodding his head towards a smooth round formation.

"Um, yeah, I guess."

Moments later, you're over the finish line.

Sidney swims toward you, looking relieved. "I was beginning to get worried. Did something happen?"

You show him your backpack. "The clam got my backpack, but a turtle rider helped me escape. See, it's hardly damaged. The straps are just a bit shorter."

Sidney's eyes gleam in admiration. "Wow, sounds like you had a bigger adventure than me."

Squee swims up to you, giving you a big dolphin smile. "Open your backpack," she says. "I have a surprise."

From beneath her flipper, she produces a large pearl.

"Everyone who completes the Round the Coral Peninsula Extravaganza gets a prize."

"That's amazing. Thank you."

"I got one too," says Sidney. "Imagine the new bikes we can get now."

"Yeah." You nod. "But first we have to get back to Mystic Portal."

"We can arrange that for you," Squee says.

"Goodbye," calls Sheriff Kingpin, entwining his blue tail around Kampos' yellow one.

"Good luck with your little seahorses," you call.

Hippo butts you with his nose. "Come back soon, right?"

In a flash of blue light, you're on the beach, with Sidney and Tracey, standing next to your bikes.

"Hey." Tracey waves. "I explored a sunken ship with the turtles. It was really dangerous, but we got out okay. How was your race?"

"We jumped squid hurdles and raced through snapping clams." Sidney grins. "And we each got these." He pulls his pearl out of his backpack.

Tracey's eyes boggle. "Wow, that's bigger than a tennis ball. You could buy hundreds of top quality bikes with that."

"That's the first thing I'm going to get." You grin. "But for now, let's take these bikes for another spin down Mystic Portal."

Congratulations, you've travelled down Mystic Portal, been for a ride on a dolphin and a seahorse, and escaped a squid and the snapping clams. But have you survived a sandstorm? Met a track-keeper? Found the You Say Which Way library? Been on a magic carpet? Or been transformed into a furry creature?

It's time to make a decision. You have 3 choices. Do you:

Go back and take a Terrific Turtle Tour? **P108**

Go to the list of choices and start reading from another part of the story? **P248**

Or

Go back to the beginning a try another path? **P1**

Return to the bazaar

"There's nothing out there." You wave towards the empty desert.

"I agree," says Tracey. "We came here to get away from the desert, we don't want to go back out there and die in that heat."

"Going back is dangerous," says Daania. "There's a magic gateway out in the desert that can get you home, but if we go back, the bandits will probably kill you."

"I don't care," says Tracey. "I'm tired and we've been in the hot sun all day. Can't we go back and have a rest in the tent? Surely there's somewhere we can hide from those horrible bandits."

"There may be one place we can hide…" Daania scratches her head. "But you'll have to be really quiet."

Daania tells the carpet to go back towards the bazaar. It bucks and sways as if it's reluctant to follow her orders, but she finally soothes it. Soon, you're near the market place. The carpet sneaks across the sand, barely above ground level so it's not visible behind the tents.

It's quite handy, not walking, because the carpet is much quieter than your feet would have been.

Behind the plain brown tent, Daania gets off the carpet, putting a finger to her lips to remind you both to stay silent. She lifts a small flap at the rear of the tent and crawls inside. You and Tracey follow.

In the dim light, you see sleeping mats on the floor and a bed along one side of the tent.

Daania's grandmother is in the bed, coughing, under mounds of stripy cotton blankets. Daania gestures that you and Tracey should hide under the bed. Tugging some blankets so they hang over the side of the bed, Daania crawls in after you.

Not a moment too soon. Boots stomp up to the tent. The fabric walls shake as the flimsy fabric door is flung open.

A male voice yells. Objects crash to the floor as they search the tent.

Tracey grips your arm. Heart pounding, you freeze, barely breathing. If they hear you…

The boots get closer to the bed. Someone barks at Daania's grandmother. She coughs as she replies. Will they search under the bed?

At last the boots start to tromp towards the door. On your arm, Tracey's grip tightens. Why is she freaking out, now? The bandits are about to leave.

Suddenly, Tracey sneezes.

A cry comes from the tent entrance. Boots pound towards the bed. The blankets are flung back.

A man looks under the bed, brandishing his sword. "Got you! Hey boss, I've got another slave to work at Sands of Time Industries."

Sorry, this part of your story is over. Going back to the bazaar led you into the hands of the bandits. They kidnap you and take you to work in a factory making magical hour glasses that slow time to a snail's pace. Unfortunately, your aging process doesn't slow, so you become wrinkled and old in no time at all. But, never mind, you can have another adventure on Mystic Portal. There are other exciting jumps that take you to strange worlds. You could transform into a furry orange creature, ride a giant turtle or meet an ogre.

It's time to make a decision. You have 3 choices. Do you:

Go back and fly the magic carpet straight ahead to get home? **P174**

Go to the list of choices and start reading from another part of the story? **P248**

Or

Go back to the beginning a try another path? **P1**

Leave the track-keepers and join Tracey

"You're right, Sidney." You frown. "It's not fair to let Tracey get upset. We'd better go back and join her."

Sidney waves his arm towards the snake bridge. "When will the skinny be ready?"

Sharmeena shrugs. "Jumps need to weather in the sun and rain before they're ready. One day when you come back, this snake will be ready and then you can try it out. In the meantime, go and enjoy our other jumps."

"Thanks," you both say.

In a flash of orange light, your body changes back into your own. Your orange fur has disappeared. Instead, you're wearing mountain biking gear, sitting astride your bike.

The snake jump is nowhere to be seen and neither are the track-keepers.

Sidney's standing by the side of the track, holding his bike.

"Hey," he calls, "you look much better with two eyes than one!"

"So do you. That was crazy. Do you think we've gone nuts? Or is there really a snake jump being built somewhere around here?"

Sidney shrugs. "If there is, it's invisible now. But I'm so glad I can't see any ogres. Come on, let's catch up to Tracey."

Congratulations, you've taken a crazy mountain bike jump, stumbled into an alternate reality, escaped an ogre and made friends with the track-keepers, the secret sculptors of Mystic Portal. When you and Sidney catch up to Tracey, she insists she's had wild adventures too. You all vow to come back to Mystic Portal another day and try out more jumps. Maybe you'd like to go on an underwater trip with Terrific Turtle Tours, fight desert bandits, ride a magic carpet or skip through snapping clams on the back of a seahorse.

It's time to make a decision. Do you:

Go back and finish building the snake bridge? **P168**

Go to the list of choices and start reading from another part of the story? **P248**

Or

Go back to the beginning a try another path? **P1**

Save Junior from the shark

Junior was trying to save you. You can't let the shark eat him.

"Hey, shark!" You wave your arms, trying to distract the shark, so it'll drop Junior.

It doesn't work.

"There." Tracey points to the loose planks. "Grab one. I'll tug the shark's fin to distract it."

Diving through the water, you grab a plank and swim back to the shark.

It's still shaking Junior from side to side, like a dog worrying a bone. Tracey is straddling the shark's back, yanking its dorsal fin.

You bring the plank down on the shark's head as hard as you can. But you're pushing through water. It's not the same as air. Your aim goes off.

Instead of hitting the shark's head, the plank smacks its nose.

The shark's jaws fly open and Junior tumbles out.

"Aagh, my nose," bellows the shark. "My sensitive nose."

You and Tracey swim to a porthole, dragging Junior through the water by his leash. You push Junior out the porthole. "Go Tracey, help him get to the surface."

She slips out the porthole.

Out of the corner of your eye, there's a flash of white.

The shark! You push your head and shoulders through the porthole, and shove off with your arms, propelling yourself outside, just as the shark's teeth graze your leg.

Pain lances though your calf and your blood floats through the water. Your leg has been bitten. You'd better get to shore before more predators smell your blood and come looking for lunch.

Heart pounding and leg throbbing, you make for the surface.

Above you, Tracey is swimming upwards, towing Junior by his seaweed leash. He's so large. How is she managing?

Something nudges you from below.

No. Another shark. You kick harder, determined to get away.

"Hold still," snaps a familiar voice. "How can I get you on my shell if you keep kicking me in the head?"

Tuck! You relax and let the turtle lift you to the surface.

Tracey is astride Nip, gripping Junior's leash. Junior floats beside her, his eyes shut. He's so peaceful, so quiet, so unlike Junior.

"He's such a sweet turtle," says his mother, Nip. "How we'll miss him."

"He was valiant," you say. "A shark attacked and he gave his life to save mine. I'm sorry."

What's that? Did Junior just move his head?

His head moves again.

He's not dead, although his eyes are still shut. No one else seems to have noticed that he's still alive. They're too busy talking and swimming.

He opens an eye and winks at you.

Ah, he's playing a trick on his parents. You decide to go along with it.

"Let's get you tourists safely to shore," says Tuck, "before that shark comes after us. Nip, have you got any healing weed?"

Nip pulls her head into her shell, then pokes it out again, holding a piece of yellow seaweed in her mouth.

"Wrap that around your injured leg," says Tuck.

Taking the weed from Nip's mouth, you bind your leg with it. Your shark bite stops bleeding. The throbbing in your leg dies down.

"Take the weed off now," says Tuck, "then rinse it, and give it back to Nip."

"But I've only had it on for a moment."

"That's all you need."

He's right. When you remove the binding, there's only a faint pink scar on your calf.

Tuck coughs. "You know, Junior's quite a good boy. Not sure if I ever told him that. I wanted him to take over the family business when we retired. Terrific Turtle Tours would have been his."

Junior's dad is tough. Maybe it would be good if Junior

heard a few good things about himself. "What was Junior really good at?"

Nip pipes up. "He told such wild tales. He was a great storyteller and very kind."

Tuck sighs. "A strong swimmer too. And he had the gift of the gab, why he could talk a father seahorse out of its eggs."

"Really Dad?" Junior squeals. "You love the way I talk? Oh, wow, have I got a story for you."

His parents are so pleased he's recovered, that they let him chatter as much as he likes.

"The shark was so vicious. I knew our friend here was a goner, Dad, so I leaped right in there, diving into its jaws. You see, with its jaws full, there was no way it could eat our tourist."

"But it nearly ate you," says Tuck, his voice choked up.

"No, I was saved by these brave tourists. We really ought to reward them you know."

"Good idea," says Tuck thoughtfully. "But you saved them too, Junior. You've proven you can keep our tourists safe, so you've qualified for your passenger license."

"That's great!" you exclaim. "Could I ride home on Junior?"

"Of course." Tuck swims alongside Junior so you can hop off his shell onto his son's.

"Wow, wow, wow. My first real live passenger." Junior

is so excited that his voice is higher and squeakier than usual. "I can't believe it. I really can't. This is so cool. I really truly honestly have my passenger license. Wow, I'm qualified. It's amazing. This is absolutely fantastic. It's the best day of my life ever. And it's all because of you!"

You can't help smiling as he swims over some giant snapping clams. Tracey points out seahorses with kids on their backs, zipping in and out of the clam shells.

"Is that the Round the Coral Peninsula Extravaganza?" you ask.

"Sure is," says Junior.

The seahorses are fast, popping out of the clam shells seconds before they shut.

"Oh no, look!" A kid's backpack straps are stuck in a clam shell. The kid struggles, but the straps only pull tighter. "Come on, Junior, let's help that kid."

Junior plunges downward. You extract a pocketknife from your backpack and cut the kid's straps free.

"Thank you." The kid grins. "You saved my life."

"No problem," you say. "I'll see you around Mystic Portal."

Junior swims back to Nip and Tuck and you all head back to the Terrific Turtle Tours' hangout, by the seaweed. Tuck disappears into the seaweed, through a patch of sunlight that makes the golden flowers glint among the seaweed.

Strange. Even though Tuck's sometimes a little

grumpy, you'd expected him to say goodbye.

You pat Junior's shell. "Thanks for the tour, Junior, and thank you for saving my life."

"Will you come back and play again?" says Junior. "That was fun. Scary, but fun."

"It's been great," says Tracey to Nip and Junior. "You've taken good care of us."

Tuck swims out of the seaweed, holding strands of weed with golden flowers in his mouth.

"How sweet, Tuck." Tracey smiles. "You brought us some flowers."

You take the stems from Tuck's mouth. The blossoms are strange, perfectly round and flat, tied onto the seaweed. "What? These aren't flowers. They're gold coins."

"I know." Tuck grins. "The seaweed is a great hiding place for the pirate treasure, isn't it?"

You and Tracey laugh.

"You saved our son's life," says Nip. "Even though he is fully grown, he's the only child we have. Please accept our small gift in return."

Congratulations, you and Tracey use your gold coins to buy new bikes for you and Sidney – and more bikes for the school mountain biking club, so other kids can go riding too. You often return to Mystic Portal to have more adventures. Maybe you'd like to join the Round the

Coral Peninsula Extravaganza, see what happens if you don't save Junior, ride a magic carpet or meet an ogre. Or you may prefer to build mountain bike jumps, or try your luck on Camel Hump or Ogre Jaws.

It's time to make a decision. You have 3 choices. Do you:

Go back and flee from the shark with Tracey? **P135**

Go to the list of choices and start reading from another part of the story? **P248**

Or

Go back to the beginning a try another path? **P1**

The Hydropolis Underwater City Tour

"It's a hard choice," you say, "but I like the sound of the thrills in the underwater city, so let's go there."

"Great, great, Hydropolis is my favorite!" Junior spins around in a circle, trying to nip his tail, churning up bubbles in the water and creating a mini whirlpool.

"Settle down, Junior!" snaps Tuck, "or we'll have to leave you behind."

"Please don't, sir," you interject. Junior will be much more fun than his parents. "We'd love to have him along. It's important that he completes his training so he can get his passenger license."

"Good point," says Nip.

Still spinning in his whirlpool, Junior winks at you.

"Oh, all right," Tuck concedes. "He can come along, but he'll have to behave himself."

Flipping out of his swirling water, Junior straightens up, as if he's standing at attention in an army inspection. "Yes, sir. I won't disappoint you."

"That's to be seen," says Tuck. He turns and swims off with Tracey on his back.

"Um, this way." Junior follows him, waving you forward with one of his forelegs.

Nip chuckles as she swims behind them. Vibrations run through her shell, tickling your legs, but you're glad she's laughing. You don't want her to be grumpy with

Junior. He's more fun than Tuck.

You eye the uneven edge of Nip's shell where a chunk is missing. "How did you chip your shell?"

"Shark bite, but I swam off, so it only got a mouthful of shell."

Sharks? You look around, but can't see any — unless they're hiding in the seaweed. "How far to Hydropolis?"

"Not far. Just a few more yards."

What's she talking about? There's only blue ocean and fish ahead. Oh, and Tuck, Tracey and Junior.

Without warning, Tuck and Junior dive downwards, disappearing from sight with Tracey.

"It's the drop off, my favorite part." Nip plunges over the edge of a coral-encrusted cliff.

Below, a vast city of skyscrapers and industrial-like buildings is sprawled on the seabed. Enormous rusty bridges span gaps between rooftops. Spires are festooned with colorful weed that waves as you approach. Crumbling office blocks look like mouths with more holes than teeth, as fish swim in and out of open windows where there must've once been glass. A lobster pokes its head out of a gaping window as you pass. The tentacles of an octopus are hanging from the orifices of a building.

Creepy. Weird. Amazing.

Landing on the roof of a skyscraper, Tuck, Tracey and Junior wait for you.

"Isn't this place awesome?" Tracey asks as you land.

"Just wait, it gets even better," squeaks Junior. "Dad, can I show them? Can I show them, please?"

Tuck nods. "Yes, son, you can."

"Follow me. Whee!" shrieks Junior, sliding down a plastic tube along the outside of the building and into a window.

Shrugging, Tracey follows. You jump after her. The chute curls and twists down the side of the building. "Hey, it's a waterslide," you call to Tracey.

She laughs.

You both erupt from the chute in a tangled mess and float above the concrete floor among darting fish.

"Look!" Junior points towards a rack of bicycles. Lobsters hold the bikes in place, each with one enormous pincher grasped around the frame and another around the bike rack. "This is best part of the Hydropolis tour." Junior beams. "Choose one and hop on."

Tracey pats a lobster on the head. "Thank you for taking care of this bike. I'd like to ride it now please." She's using her polite voice – good call. Those lobsters' pincers look pretty sharp.

You choose a bike at the other end of the rack, thank a lobster, and get on. "Hey, this is unusual. I've never been on a floating bike before." No matter how hard you grip the handlebars, your butt floats off the bike seat, and your feet don't want to stay on the pedals.

"Fasten your seatbelt," laughs Junior. "And put your feet in the pedal clips." He picks up a long flat object in his mouth and swims over to you.

"What's that?"

"Mff, mff ivvnning mrrfff."

You can't understand him, because of the thing in his mouth.

"A diving belt," says Tracey. "It has lead in it to stop you floating to the surface."

Once you and Tracey secure your belts, seatbelts and pedal clips, Junior swims out a window and you follow. Pedaling the bike turns a propeller on the back, which moves you through the water. "Hey, this is cool."

A purple fish swims past your face, turning its bulbous yellow eyes towards you. It darts away to join a school of other purple fish, moving in unison like they all know the same dance.

Junior leads you to the rooftop of another building. "Visitors from Mystic Portal often enjoy biking," he says. "They tell us these bridges are the best feature of the city, and often want to bike over them. Follow me." He takes off across the rooftop, then swims just above the surface of a bridge.

"Let's go," calls Tracey, biking off after him, her propeller leaving a trail of bubbles that stream past as you follow her.

This is great. The propeller provides extra power,

shooting you across the roof of the building and up over the high arc of the bridge. The ironwork on the bridge's rails is rusty and hung with streamers of seaweed. At the highest point of the bridge, you fly high into the water, then float down, landing next to Tracey and Junior.

"This is incredible. We should try some directional jumps too."

Tracey nods. "Brilliant idea. With the combination of a propeller and water, directional jumps should work well."

"Let's do a team jump," you say. "I'll go left, you go right."

You and Tracey race side-by-side up an arched bridge. At the peak, you twist your handlebars and lean to the left. Your bike follows, floating effortlessly through the water.

Tracey has veered to the right. You land on buildings at the opposite ends of a narrow flat bridge. Hunkering down on your bike, you tighten your seatbelt and pedal like crazy. Tracey's doing the same. There's no room to pass each other. It's a classic game of chicken. Which one of you will give way first?

You keep your eyes ahead. Tracey's getting closer. And closer. Too close. You're about to crash. Yanking your handlebars vertically, you lean back, pedaling hard. Your bike speeds up towards the surface. Tracey does the same.

Her laughter drifts on the current. You push your bike

back into a horizontal position and circle round to meet each other. You experiment with your water bikes, dodging in and out of buildings, somersaulting over obstacles and pedaling around abandoned factories. Junior makes sure you don't go near the octopus' lair, just in case it attacks.

Soon Nip and Tuck arrive to guide you back.

"This has been awesome," says Tracey "I've learned so many new skills, so much about balance. You can't always test that stuff on land, because you'd hurt yourself."

"Yeah." You can't help grinning. "It would have been too risky to try these stunts on Mystic Portal."

"Can we come back again?" Tracey's eyes are pleading. "Please?"

"Of course you can," says Junior. "Oh, I mean, can they, Mom? Dad?"

"Sure," says Tuck. "You've given Junior some good practice at tour guiding today."

"But how will we find you?" Tracey asks.

"That's easy," you answer. "We'll go down Mystic Portal and over Dolphin Slide again."

"Can you come again tomorrow?" asks Junior, wagging his tail.

"We'll come again as soon as we can," you assure him. "We love it here, don't we, Tracey?"

The turtles swim to the edge of the shore.

"Thank you," you and Tracey call as you climb out of the sea onto the soft white sand.

"Hey, look." Tracey points at your bikes, leaning against a tree at the edge of the sand.

"Hey, how were the turtles?" Sidney calls, emerging from the water. "I had a blast on the seahorses."

"Hydropolis is an incredible underwater city," calls Tracey. "You'll have to come with us next time."

"Sure will," says Sidney, wringing out the dripping hem of his shirt. "Let's come back tomorrow. There are so many cool things to do on this trail."

"I can't wait." You grin as Tracey, you and Sidney high-five each other.

Congratulations, you and Tracey often return to Hydropolis underwater city, bringing Sidney with you. You all become so good at jumping and bike tricks that you become the best bike acrobatics team in your area. Sponsors clamor to provide you with the latest fanciest mountain bikes and biking gear. You keep your old bike, just for fun. Often, you take a quick trip down Mystic Portal with Tracey and Sidney to try out the new jumps that mysteriously appear on the trail. There are many more adventures on Mystic Portal. You could visit the sunken ship, ride a seahorse in the Round the Coral Peninsula Extravaganza, ride a magic carpet, face bandits, or tame an ogre. The choice is yours.

It's time to make a decision. Do you:

Go back and ride a seahorse in the Round the Coral Peninsula Extravaganza? **P97**

Go to the list of choices and start reading from another part of the story? **P248**

Or

Go back to the beginning a try another path? **P1**

Return to ride Mystic Portal

The ground trembles beneath your feet. Usually you'd think it was an earthquake, but now you know it's Bog. Your fur stinks of smoke and the bright daylight up here makes your eye squint.

Sidney leans in and whispers, "I don't fancy getting caught by Bog again. What say we go for another bike ride?"

"Good idea," you mutter as the ground quivers again. "The sooner we get back on our bikes, the better." You turn to Sharmeena. "Thanks so much for saving us from Bog. It would be fun to build trails, but we're pretty tired right now, so maybe we could come another day."

She nods and blinks her large eye at you. "I'll be here, building more jumps. Feel free to join me anytime you want." She vanishes in a flash of orange light.

Suddenly you're standing on the side of the track, holding your bike. Sidney's next to you, taking a swig of water from his drink bottle. His bike's leaning against the trunk of a nearby pine.

What just happened? Did you imagine everything? Are you going crazy? Or are there really strange creatures running around beneath the track?

You clear your throat awkwardly.

Sidney's eyes dart around as if he's expecting Bog to charge out of the trees.

"Um…" You clear your throat again.

You're just downhill from Ogre Jaws. There doesn't appear to be anything odd lurking in the trees, but something strange is hanging off the back of Sidney's bike.

Walking over, you reach out and touch the orange fluffy tail dangling from his seat post. "I guess we didn't just imagine everything."

"Look, you've got one too," says Sidney, pointing at another orange tail on the back of your bike. He looks relieved. "I thought I was going nuts, but now I know I'm fine."

"Fine?" You laugh. "We're back on the bike trail, alive, with cool tails. That's better than fine. It's great."

"Beats being stuck in a cage with a fire-breathing ogre waiting to eat you," says Sidney, shuddering.

"Sure does." You get back on your bike. "Let's do some more jumps. I'm dying to see what happens next."

With a thrum of tires, Tracey bursts out of the trees. She's just come down the chicken line around Ogre Jaws.

"Hey, am I glad to see you two!" Her bike skids to a stop. "I had the craziest adventure. When I went over Camel Hump, my bike turned into a magic carpet. I've been battling desert bandits and I even met a genie from a magic lamp."

There are long gold and green threads wound around Tracey's handlebars. Could they be from the magic carpet?

"Sounds like fun," says Sidney, "but we've been fighting an ogre!"

"Fighting an ogre? Stop teasing me," groans Tracey. "I'm serious."

"So are we," says Sidney.

You nod. "He's telling the truth."

"Yeah, right," Tracey rolls her eyes then stares at the orange tails on your bikes. "Wow!" She raises an eyebrow. "Let's go. I want to see what happens on our next jump."

Congratulations. You saved Sidney from an ogre, became a track-keeper and cut your way through rock with a laser beam. Every chance you have, you come back to Mystic Portal. The track is never the same twice and each jump takes you to a new adventure. You may like to build a new jump with the track-keepers, go on Tracey's magic carpet, meet a talking camel or visit the underwater city of Hydropolis.

It's time to make a decision. Do you:

Go back and stay with the track-keeper to build new jumps? **P88**

Go to the list of choices and start reading from another part of the story? **P248**

Or

Go back to the beginning a try another path? **P1**

Finish building the snake bridge

"Tracey's used to us disappearing and hiding from her," you say.

"That's true," says Sidney. "Maybe we can stay a few more minutes and finish off this bridge."

"Team," calls Sharmeena, "finish the landing ramp and snake bridge while I take our friends to get some water."

"But we're not thirsty." The last thing you want is to miss is jump building. It usually takes months to make a jump. These cool track-keepers are doing this jump in an hour or two.

"This time, the water is not to drink. Well, it is in a way." Sharmeena laughs. "Come on, I'll show you what I mean."

You go back to the river and Sharmeena bends down and starts drinking. And drinking. And drinking! At her throat, the fur swells, creating a huge bulge.

"Wow," says Sidney, "you're just like a pelican, with a pouch that swells up when it's full of fish. Only yours is for water."

Sharmeena motions with her foreleg for you to do the same. You and Sidney bend down to drink. It's amazing how much water your pouch can hold. A huge bulge swells out under your fur so you can hardly see your hooves.

You both follow Sharmeena back to the new launch

ramp. She spits water all over the jump.

"Come on," she says. "Every jump needs to be weathered with the rain and sun to make it hard enough for bikes to go over it. This speeds up the process."

You and Sidney spit your water over the ramp too. Once you're finished, track-keepers stomp all over the ramp to compact it. Racing back to the river, the three of you gather more water for the off-ramp, then join in, stomping down the damp earth.

"Can't wait to jump this," says Sidney, "but it won't be ready for months. What a shame we don't have a giant hairdryer to dry it all out and make it hard."

"Yeah," you answer, "or a whole month of scorching hot days."

"We have something better," says Sharmeena. "Hide over here, and watch."

A group of track-keepers carry a bundle of silver ropes in their teeth. They stand on the track just down from the off-ramp and spread out, tugging the ropes. It's a silver net. How is that going to harden the jumps and make them more stable? Maybe it's for bikers who fall off? No, the net is placed *after* the bridge, not under it.

Sidney elbows you. "What are they doing?" He frowns.

A thunderous roar echoes through the trees.

"Quick," says Sharmeena. "Deep breath. Use your camouflage."

Together, you and Sidney take enormous breaths and

are instantly camouflaged.

A moment later, Bog crashes out of the trees, chasing a tiny track-keeper. The wee creature runs, flat out, its orange fur ruffling in the wind. Bog stomps along behind it, bellowing.

"Can't catch me," calls the tiny one, racing up the on-ramp.

Roaring, Bog blasts the little track-keeper with an enormous jet of flame.

But the little one leaps high in the air, clearing the huge gap where the snake bridge will go, and scampering down the off-ramp.

With another ear-splitting roar that makes your knees tremble, Bog leaps over the gap and blasts fire at the off-ramp. He charges after the tiny track-keeper, who nimbly ducks in and out of the silver net. The other track-keepers discard their camouflage and they pull the ropes tight around Bog.

"No, not net. I hate nets," Bog cries as the ropes ensnare him. His writhes in the net, trapped.

Sharmeena steps forward. "We won't use the net on you again, Bog, if you promise to harden our jumps with your fire and to stop chasing us."

"But I so hungry," says Bog. "You so tasty. Takes lot of food to feed big guy like me. You let my human toast go." He starts to cry.

Poor Bog, its sounds like he's having a rough time.

Beside you, Sidney mutters, "Can't fool me. He'd try to eat me again if he had a chance."

"That's no excuse, Bog," says Sharmeena. "If you help us build these tracks for humans to play on, we can bring you plenty of vegetables to eat, but you have to promise to stop hunting people and track-keepers."

Bog's Mohawk is crushed, and his skin is red and inflamed from the net.

"I bet that net's enchanted," you whisper to Sidney.

"Looks like it," he says.

Bog stops crying. "Yes. Anything to stop the net."

"We'll let you lose, now," says Sharmeena. "But you have to prove your loyalty by lifting that snake bridge onto this jump and making sure it's secure."

Bog wipes his nose, leaving globs of snot on his arm, then nods.

Moments later, the bridge is in place. The ogre stomps on the ends, pressing them deep into the ramps so the bridge doesn't wobble. He shoots jets of flame over the surface of the dirt to harden it.

The track-keepers cheer, and praise him.

Bog stands back to admire his work. A tear glints in his eye. "I never... um... never made anything before," he says. "I only destroyed things." He pats the tiny track-keeper on the head. "Never had friends before."

Bog comes over to Sidney and grins. "Sorry about toast. We be friends too?"

"Sure." Sidney gulps. "Um, no problem, I think." Only a few hours ago, he was going to be Bog's human toast. You don't blame him for freaking. "Um, I like your hair." He points at Bog's red Mohawk.

"Thank you." Bog's stomach growls.

The track-keepers laugh. "Let's get you some vegetables now, shall we?" says Sharmeena. "Before you get too hungry..."

Great idea. Neither you nor Sidney want him to eat you or your new friends.

"Yummy," Bog says. "I roast them?"

"Sidney," Tracey's voice yells through the trees. "Where are you two?"

"We'd better get back to Tracey." You wave to Bog, Sharmeena and the other track-keepers. "We'll see you again soon."

In a flash of orange light, you're suddenly both human, on your bikes again, riding along the track behind Tracey.

"Hey, Tracey," you call out. "Where have you been? We've been looking for you for hours."

"I went down Camel Hump." Tracey stops at the side of the track. "Wait until you hear where Camel Hump took me." She grins. "What have you two been up to?"

You and Sidney exchange a glance. Whatever happened to her, she's never going to believe your story.

Congratulations, you escaped Bog and made friends with him, met the secret track-keepers, and helped build a new feature on Mystic Portal. You could ride a magic carpet, fight desert bandits or ride a seahorse. You could also find the track-keepers' secret library, visit a sunken ship or win some gold.

It's time to make a decision. Do you:

Go back and try to use Bog's key to free Sidney? **P57**

Go to the list of choices and start reading from another part of the story? **P248**

Or

Go back to the beginning a try another path? **P1**

Fly the magic carpet straight ahead to get home

Even though you can only see sky and sand ahead, and can't see any way of getting home, you'd rather trust Daania than those bandits. "We'll go home," you tell her. "Show us the way."

Flying over the desert, you marvel at the ripples and patterns in the sand far below.

"Beautiful, isn't it?" asks Daania. "Those patterns are caused by the wind."

"Incredible," says Tracey. "Not a camel's hoof print in sight."

The desert seems to stretch on forever, endless dunes merging with the sky on the horizon.

"What are those blobs over there?" Tracey leans forward, shading her eyes with her hand.

"Those are rocks," answers Daania. The carpet zooms closer. "See that big one with the arch?"

"You mean the one that looks like an elephant?" you ask.

"Exactly," says Daania "it's called elephant rock. That's where we're heading."

The enormous reddish-brown rock rises out of the desert plateau. Other large rocks are scattered nearby. Its resemblance to an elephant is so uncanny you almost imagine its ear twitching. One end of the rock is similar to an elephant's head, with a hollow where its eye would be. A thick trunk runs from its head down into the ground.

Daania points to the space between the trunk and the body. "We're going through there," she says. "If the carpet flies under the elephant's trunk, anyone on it will instantly go home. Well, that's what local legends say."

"Legends?" questions Tracey, her voice trembling. "We're relying on an old legend?"

You place your hand on her shoulder. "Just like legends of magic carpets," you say, "and talking camels. Now we know they're true too."

Tracey grins. "Yeah, we're the stuff of legends, now!" She taps Daania on the shoulder. "If this works, I'm happy to leave the carpet with you. Take good care of it, and remember: always speak to it nicely."

Daania's eyes shine with tears. "Thank you," she says. "My grandmother needs an operation in hospital, but she's too old to go by camel. Now I can take her on the carpet." She kisses Tracey's cheek. "I promise to take care of it, until you both return."

"Thanks Daania."

Elephant rock looms in front of you. "Look," you cry, pointing at the shimmering air under the trunk. "That looks really weird."

"It's your gateway home." Daania smiles. "Have a nice trip."

You and Tracey barely have time to call, "Thank you,"

before the carpet zips under the elephant's trunk.

With a whump, you're both back on your bikes, riding down the lower part of Mystic Portal. Sidney's shirt flashes on the trail ahead of you.

"Hey, Sidney," you call. "Wait up."

He stops his bike. "Man, I thought I'd lost you both," he says when you catch up. "What's that on your wheels?"

You and Tracey look down. "Wow," murmurs Tracey, winking at you. Twisted around your spokes are gold and green threads from the magic carpet.

Sidney would never believe your adventure. "Oh, that's um…," you say, trying to improvise like crazy.

Tracey saves the day. "Dunno. Must've come from that sandy patch we rode through."

You laugh out loud. She's right. You *did* ride a camel and a magic carpet through a *sandy* patch – an enormous patch of the Sahara desert!

Sidney looks puzzled. "I didn't see any sand," he says.

"That's because you went down the chicken line," you answer.

"By the way," says Tracey, "did you see any chickens? After all, we saw a camel on Camel Hump."

"Ha, ha. Come on, let's get riding." Sidney jumps on his bike and you and Tracey follow him down the hill, grinning.

The next jump is tiny, hardly worth mentioning, except

when you're in the air, the tinkling laughter of the magic carpet floats up from your wheels. As if your bike has a mind of its own, it starts sweeping and loop-the-loop-ing, high above the trees.

Tracey's bike has gone wild too, somersaulting her through the air. "Yay," she cries. "Now we can be bike acrobats."

With carpet in your spokes, you'll never need a new bike. This one will always fly.

Congratulations, you survived the desert, met a talking camel, made friends with a magic carpet and Daania, and now have a new bike that flies. You could also find seahorses or an ogre, confront a sand storm, race a camel, or work for an Arab merchant.

It's time to make a decision. You have 3 choices. Do you:

See what happens if you return to the bandits at the bazaar? **P145**

Go to the list of choices and start another part of the story? **P248**

Or

Go back to the beginning a try another path? **P1**

Trade the magic carpet for the lamp and genie

"Magic wishes sound awesome," you say to Tracey. "We should trade."

"I agree." Tracey hands the carpet to the girl.

The girl passes the lamp to Tracey, unrolls the carpet and climbs on, speaking to it gently in her own language. The carpet whooshes into the air. "Be careful how you use your wishes," she calls out, before she speeds off into the desert.

Tracey bites her nails, and hands the lamp to you. "You go first."

You can't believe *she's* nervous. She's always calling you and Sidney chickens. "Surely you aren't afraid of a little lamp?" you ask.

"No, I'm fine," she says, stepping away from the lamp, as if it will bite her. "Come on, rub it and see what happens."

The lamp is old-fashioned. A long spout extends from its belly with a wick set in the end of it. The top surface is carved and has a small lid for refilling the oil. The handle is warm in your hands. "Oh well, here goes," you say, polishing the tarnished gold with your fingertips.

Purple smoke wafts from the spout. The pungent smell of lavender fills the air.

"Whaddaya want?" says a grumpy voice. "Can't you see you've woken me?"

The smoke thins and a little man is standing in front of you. His ears and nose are decorated with gold rings. His purple and gold waistcoat and golden billowing trousers sparkle in the bright desert sun. Frowning, he stamps a foot, making tiny bells tinkle on the end of his pointy crimson shoes. "I said, why did you wake me?" He twirls the ends of his droopy moustache.

Tracey replies, "Daania said you'd grant us each three wishes."

"What? Daania gave me away?" The genie folds his arms. "Well, I'm having a bad hair day. I don't feel like granting any wishes."

"But you don't have any hair!" exclaims Tracey, staring at his bald brown head.

"So what! I don't have to work just because you rub my lamp and ask me to." He folds his arms and turns his back on you. "I'm striking. I'm feeling off-color."

There's nothing off-color about his bronzed skin.

"Please?" asks Tracey. "Just for us."

This is amazing. She's nearly begging. You've never seen her plead for anything before.

The genie ignores her.

Tracey's voice grows soft as she cajoles the genie. "We're terribly sorry for waking you. We don't want much," she says. "Just new bikes and to get back home. Please."

Tracey is using the P-word again. Incredible.

"Nope, I said I'm on strike." He stomps his foot again.

This is a losing battle. You have to do something. Maybe flattery will work. "All we want is to get home. Surely you can help us? After all, you're so strong and powerful."

"Sneaky tourists with their nasty tricks, flattering camels and carpets and pretending to have manners," he roars, whirling to face you. "I've had enough of you. Be gone!" The genie flings his hands outwards.

In a blinding flash of purple light and smoke, the tents disappear.

You're standing next to your bikes near the bottom of Mystic Portal. Just below you, Sidney takes a small jump and lands on the pale dunes above the beach.

He turns and waves. "Hey, where have you two been? I've been waiting for you for ages. Come on."

"Wow, that was amazing," murmurs Tracey, "but I'm glad it's over."

"Yeah, it was incredible, but what a shame that genie didn't grant us any wishes."

"Well, at least we survived." Tracey gestures at the track. "After you."

Tracey's letting you go first? Unheard of. Perhaps she learned some manners in the desert, after all.

"Thanks." You get on your bike, wondering if you dreamed everything.

A high tingling laugh rings through the forest. The

carpet? No, you can't see a flying mat anywhere. Until you glance at your handlebars and notice tattered threads of gold and green carpet twirled around them.

You take the small jump at the bottom of the track. Maybe, just maybe, the genie did grant one of your wishes. "Take me home please," you say.

Instead of landing, your bike the veers to the left and heads through the sky towards home.

Laughing, Tracey instructs her bike to do the same.

Upon the white dunes far below, Sidney stares at you both, his mouth hanging open. "Hey," he calls, "wait for me."

Tracey laughs again. "Dear carpet," she says, "Could you help Sidney?" She takes a strand of carpet off her handlebars and throws it down to Sidney. "Wrap this around your bike."

Sidney catches the thread and winds it around his frame. Moments later, he's in the air beside you. "Hey," he calls, "Mystic Portal is the best!"

Congratulations. You survived the desert, taught Tracey to be more pleasant, met a talking camel and flew on a magic carpet. Although the genie didn't directly grant your wish, he did send you and Tracey home, and gave your bikes new powers – mountain biking will never be the same again. Maybe you'd like to take some of the other exciting jumps on Mystic Portal. Who knows what new worlds are down the track waiting to be explored?

It's time to make a decision. You have 3 choices. Do you:

Go back to the bazaar and keep the magic carpet? **P41**

Go to the list of choices and start reading from another part of the story? **P248**

Or

Go back to the beginning a try another path? **P1**

Go to the track-keeper party

"Let's party!" you and Sidney cry.

"Great!" Sharmeena bounds down the right-hand tunnel, jostling you and Sidney on her back. Her green light beam bounces off the walls.

At the back of your mind is a nagging worry. Bog is happy now with his belly full, but what will happen when he gets hungry again? You and Sidney don't have any more peanut butter and jelly. Although you promised Bog you'd teach the track-keepers how to make it, what if they don't have the ingredients?

After a few minutes, the passage leads to an enormous cavern. Green lights around the walls illuminate a large crowd of track-keepers, chatting, playing leapfrog and doing gymnastics.

"Wow, there are so many of you," Sidney exclaims. "I thought there might be a few track-keepers, but not hundreds."

He's right. There are way more than you'd imagined.

Sharmeena leaps onto a small stage in the front of the cabin and lets out a shrill whistle. The hubbub ceases. All the track-keepers turn to face you. Still on Sharmeena's back behind you, Sidney grips your waist even tighter.

Sharmeena raises her voice so it carries throughout the cavern. "These two adventurers have tamed Bog. They discovered he was only fierce because he was hungry, and they found food that satisfies him.''

Cheers and whistles ring through the cavern. Track-keepers stomp their hooves. Others do somersaults in midair, the green beams of their eyes ricocheting around the room. You can't help grinning. Sidney's grip on your waist relaxes and he lets out a whoop.

"Party! Party!" The track-keepers chant.

But then it hits you again – Bog could attack at any moment.

Dismounting, you stride to the front of the stage and hold your hand high. Soon the mayhem stops and the track-keepers are silent, watching you. Except for one small track-keeper, who keeps whistling and bouncing around.

"We may have tamed Bog for now," you say, "but I'm afraid we haven't solved your problem." An undercurrent of murmurs runs through the cavern. Clearing your throat, you continue. "Bog will need more peanut butter and jelly. I doubt you have any and I don't know how we're going to make it."

To your surprise, the little wriggly track-keeper laughs. "No problem," it squeals, turning another somersault.

"But–"

Low chuckles break out, then giggles and loud raucous laughter. Some of the creatures roll around the floor. Sharmeena is cracking up too.

Sidney nudges you. "What's so funny?"

"I don't know." You shrug. "Maybe they're delirious with fear, but Bog will eat them if we can't make peanut butter and jelly."

The laughing crowd parts to let a group of track-keepers through. They're dragging something fastened to two long ropes. As they get closer, you see that it's a huge earthenware pot, mounted on wheels.

Sharmeena whistles to quiet the crowd, then turns to you. "This is why we're laughing."

An ominous roar floats down the tunnel.

Bog! He could be here any minute. "You think a piece of pottery is going to stop an ogre?" you cry. "It's not even big enough to block the cavern door. And even if it was, he'd shatter it in moments. How is this going to help?"

Sharmeena smiles. "Take the lid off."

Lifting the lid, you peer inside. "It's empty." How disappointing. Bog roars again. "I wish it was full of peanut butter," you say, shooting a nervous glance towards the corridor. "That would solve our problem."

Around you, track-keepers start laughing again, pounding the floor with their hooves. You're about to snap something rude at Sharmeena when you smell the delicious aroma of peanut butter and raspberry jelly. Your nostrils flare. Your nose twitches.

Sidney is sniffing the air, too. "Is that what I'd think it is?" He points at the pot.

It's full to overflowing with peanut butter, shot through with beautiful thick swirls of raspberry jelly.

"Impossible," you murmur.

"No it's not." Sharmeena laughs. "The pot of plenty makes sure we have whatever food we wish for. If we'd only known that Bog was hungry, we could have fed him."

"Yum." Sidney scoops a fistful of peanut butter and jelly out of the pot, and licks it off his hand.

"Ew, yuck, Sidney." You wrinkle your nose. "No one will want to eat out of the pot now that your hand's been in it."

"Except me!" booms a voice from the door of the cavern.

You gulp. It's Bog, looking meaner than ever in the eerie green glow of the cavern. His red Mohawk bristles and his nostrils flare.

Then he grins and races towards the pot, sticking his face inside to suck out the peanut butter and jelly. Moments later, the pot is empty. Bog's face is covered in smears of peanut butter and blobs of jelly. He burps happily. "Someone say party here?" he asks.

"Lights," calls Sharmeena.

The green lights around the edge of the cavern pulse. Only they're not lights at all – they're track-keepers, using their eyes as lights, blinking in rhythm with one another.

Sidney raises his eyebrows. "Wow, these creatures are

handy."

"Drums." Sharmeena claps her hands.

A ring of track-keepers stomp their hooves, creating a drumbeat.

"Music," she calls.

Track-keepers start to sing bizarre yodeling songs with a catchy beat. You can't stop your feet from tapping in time to the music.

"Dancers," Sharmeena yells over the music.

Track-keepers somersault through the air, and land in formation. They twirl and jump to the music.

Sharmeena nods at you. "Get on."

You climb upon her back and hang on for dear life as she leaps among the dancers. Your adrenaline surges. Exhilaration flows through you. This party is in your honor. You saved Sidney and the track-keepers from Bog.

Bog surges into the crowd, heading your way. He scoops you off Sharmeena's back and flings you into the air. With a whump, you land in his arms and he hoists you onto his shoulders.

"My hero," he sings at the top of his rich bass voice. "You brought peanut butter and jelly, oh so lovely and smelly, so I can fill my belly."

Amazing. Whoever thought that ogres could sing?

You dance for hours, and then you and Sidney flop onto some large cushions in a corner.

"Let's try out the pot of plenty," says Sidney, eyes gleaming. Before you can stop him, he says, "I wish for chocolate brownies."

The aroma of warm chocolaty brownies wafts from the pot. Grabbing a handful, you both munch them down.

"I wish for curry," says Sidney.

The brownies disappear and a spicy scent fills the air, making your belly grumble – although you've just eaten.

"That wasn't very clever." You roll your eyes at Sidney. "We don't have any cutlery."

"That's okay." He reaches for the pot. "We'll just drink the curry down."

No he won't. "I wish for candy."

The jar is immediately filled with all sorts of sweets in brightly-colored wrappers.

You only have a chance to take one, before Sidney calls, "I wish for kumara fries."

"What's kumara?" You peer inside the pot.

Small wedges of orange and yellow vegetable, coated with seasoning, fill the pot. "These smell incredible," you say. "What are they?"

"Kumara," says Sidney smugly. "Sweet potato from New Zealand. It's famous all over the Internet. I've always wanted to try one."

You bite into a kumara fry. "This is the best food I've ever tasted."

"Great, isn't it?" Sidney grins. "It's a shame Tracey isn't here to enjoy these. She'd love them."

Tracey! What's happened to her while you've been underground? You'd better get back to Mystic Portal.

As if she can read your mind, Sharmeena appears beside you. "The party's winding down, so you'll need to go home," she says, "but because you've helped us, we'd like to give you both a gift before you leave."

Sharmeena leads you to a small tunnel at the back of the party cavern. Her eye lights up the passage. You round a corner and come to an enormous pile of bikes.

"Careless riders abandon these on Mystic Portal. We bring them here to tidy up the litter, but we can't use them. Would you both like one?"

Litter? These bikes are top quality!

"Would we ever!" Sidney selects a bike that's the same model as Tracey's new one.

You choose a top-of-the-range mountain bike with the latest front and back suspension, high-tensile forks and mag wheels. "This is awesome. Thank you, Sharmeena."

She grins. "Follow me." Sharmeena takes you up a steep spiraling tunnel. It's so tight, your bikes just squeeze around the corners. The tunnel ends in a rocky wall. There's no way out.

"What now?"

The beam from Sharmeena's eye shoots out and hits a small red button embedded in the rock.

"Didn't notice that button," says Sidney.

The rock slides away. Outside is Mystic Portal. You and Sidney wheel your bikes out onto the trail. You both turn to Sharmeena.

"Thanks so much for the new bikes." You wave.

"Yeah, they're great." Sidney waves too.

"You deserve them for taming Bog," says Sharmeena. "See you around." The rocky door on the side of the cliff slides shut.

Tracey rounds a corner and skids to a halt in front of you. "Hey what are you two doing here? And where did you get those bikes?"

"You're never going to believe this!" says Sidney excitedly.

You shake your head. "Yeah, he's right. We've had an adventure, but it's been unbelievable!"

"Why don't you try me? I've just had a really strange ride," says Tracey. "After what happened to me, I'd believe anything!"

Congratulations, you freed Sidney and tamed Bog the ogre, keeping the track-keepers safe so they can build more jumps on Mystic Portal. You've also had a great party and have a fantastic new bike. There are plenty of other adventures on Mystic Portal. Maybe you'd like to fly on a magic carpet like Tracey, see giant pearls inside snapping clams or confront a shark. Or you could go back and see what happens if you bend the bars to free Sidney.

It's time to make a decision. Do you:

Go back and bend the bars to free Sidney? **P81**

Go to the list of choices and start reading from another part of the story? **P248**

Or

Go back to the beginning a try another path? **P1**

Stay for slingshot training

"I think we'd better stay," you say. "We'll never survive in the desert, and we don't know how to get home."

"Yeah," says Tracey. "I don't fancy being the main course for vultures."

"Or their desert dessert," you reply.

Tracey smiles. "Let's help them unload."

Although poison seems like odd cargo for schools, you have nothing better to do, so you agree to help.

As one of the guards passes Tracey a box, she stumbles, dropping it. The top flies open and plastic bottles of brightly-colored stuff spill out.

Poison must come in all shades of the rainbow. You bend down to help her pick up the bottles. "Hey!" You hold up a bottle, pointing at the label. "This isn't poison. It's poster paint!"

The guard laughs, and calls, "Hey, these kids thought we were shipping poison to school children."

Other guards join in laughing. One of them calls, "Why would we do that? My son goes to the school that these supplies are being shipped to."

"And my daughter," calls another.

Karim comes over. "I'm sorry, that must have given you a fright. I should have explained earlier. I made my fortune importing rat poison, years ago. We're just re-using these old boxes." He opens some other boxes.

"See?"

The cartons hold rubber bands, balloons, crayons, colored pencils, paper, books and other school supplies. You and Tracey grin foolishly.

"We're glad you're helping children. That's awesome." Both of you pick up boxes and follow the guards to the storage room.

After the school supplies are unloaded, a guard shows you the slingshot training area – a wide hall with tires mounted on targets at one end. An odd metal track runs along the side of the room. Children are a few yards in front of you, shooting metal darts from modern-looking slingshots. They hardly ever miss the tires.

"How are we going to get that good?" whispers Tracey.

"Dunno."

A man with a braided beard, a thick gold ring through his nose and a chest wider than a camel's, strides towards you. "New trainees?" He shakes your hands. "I'm Achmed. We'll have you shooting as well as these youngsters in no time." He nods to dismiss the guard and takes you both to a stand in a corner of the room.

Upon the stand is an ornate full-face helmet. Its polished black surface reflects your face, like a glassy lake. Crouched upon the front of the helmet is a sleek golden panther, its legs coiled with power as if it's about to leap out and devour you.

"That panther's real gold, isn't it?" asks Tracey.

Achmed nods. "24 carat."

"Wow," you breathe. The helmet's beautiful. You can't help yourself, you reach out to touch the panther.

"STOP!" shouts Achmed.

Just in time. Red laser beams spring to life, criss-crossing the area around the helmet.

Instinctively, you yank your hand back.

"You were lucky," Achmed says. "You only activated the warning system. Any further, and you would've lost your fingers. The bandits have been trying to steal this helmet for years, so we had to set up this system."

Rubbing your fingers with your other hand you stutter, "Th-thanks."

"Close call," mutters Tracey. "Are you okay?"

Achmed twists one of the braids from his beard around his finger. "This helmet will be awarded after our next battle – to the youngster who prevents the most bandits from reaching our compound."

You want that helmet. You'll do whatever it takes to get it. "How effective are the slingshots and darts?" you ask. "And how many bandits has the best kid stopped so far?"

"The slingshots are good," Achmed says, "but the bandits know we have them, and they're always coming up with ideas to outwit us. So far, we've managed to keep the bandits away from our compound by disabling their vehicles, so no one has been hurt. The best youngster has stopped four vehicles of bandits, so far this month." He points to a girl. "Bahar is our best shot," he says proudly. "She's my daughter, and will probably win the helmet."

Not if you can help it. You'd love that helmet.

"Here." He passes you and Tracey each a newfangled slingshot.

Weird. These slingshots are nothing like you've ever seen before.

Achmed shows you how to hold it by the sturdy plastic handle. It's strange, the handle goes sideways, not straight up and down like you'd imagined. It attaches to a rectangular metal frame. Yellow tubes hang off the back of the frame. A small barrel, like a gun barrel, is attached to the top of the rectangular frame, with clear plastic beneath, marked with a red cross.

You pull at the tube, saying, "We pull this to fire the darts, don't we?"

Achmed nods.

"That means the dart flies through the middle of the frame," says Tracey. "But what's this barrel on top?"

"The plastic's probably for sighting, but I don't know what the barrel does," you answer, turning to Achmed.

"That's a laser to help you sight your target accurately."

Tracey looks impressed. "Laser? That's hi-tech."

Achmed nods. "A microcomputer calculates how far

the laser is from the target, and shows you where to aim."
He waves at his daughter. "Bahar, come over and
demonstrate. You other youngsters, stand by the wall, so
you don't get hit."

Tracey and the others move aside.

Bahar is tall, about your age, with a long dark plait.
Holding the slingshot up, she pulls a dart from a pouch
at her side, fits it in the yellow tubing, and pulls it back.
"Just press this button on the handle," she says. At the
far end of the room, her green laser lights up a spot on a
tire. "Then line up your laser spot with the red cross on
the plastic sight, and release the tubing." She looks
through the clear plastic and lets go of the tubing. Her
dart hits the tire.

Achmed nods at you. "Your turn."

You miss your first few shots, but that's not so bad
because Tracey does too. After ten minutes, you're both
hitting the targets every time.

Tracey's eyes shine with pleasure. "This is so much
fun."

With a groan, the metal track along the side of the
room starts to move. A hatch opens and a cutout
wooden panel of a Land Rover moves along the rail. It
has real tires mounted where the wheels should be, and is
followed by several others.

The kids line up and shoot their darts at the moving
targets, hitting the tires. You and Tracey join the queue.

You both keep firing until your battery packs are flat and need recharging.

"Come on," says Achmed, "it's getting late and you must be famished."

After a fine feast of meat, salads, dips and flatbread smothered with herbs and goat cheese, you fall into a huge bed, exhausted. In no time, you're asleep.

In the morning, you're woken by loud rapping on the door. Tracey calls, "Quick! Get up! Bandits are coming."

You scramble out of your room and meet her in the hallway. "Here," she says, giving you your slingshot. "The batteries are fully charged."

When you're further down the hallway, Achmed calls you. "In here, come and get your armor."

Armor sounds serious. The room is crowded with guards and the slingshot crew, preparing for battle. Achmed thrusts bullet-proof vests and trousers at you and passes out sturdy grey helmets and binoculars. Bullets? No way! But, like soldiers in a war zone, you're ready in no time.

Achmed points to a burly guard. "Stick with Duba, he'll look after you."

You dash behind Duba up narrow stairs to the top of the compound wall, Tracey's feet thudding behind you. The distant whine of motors echoes across the desert. Clouds of dust billow on the horizon. Your heart pounds. The bandits will be here soon.

Tracey gives you a tight nervous smile and raises her binoculars to her eyes. "I had no idea there'd be so many. Take a look."

The drone of four-wheel drives makes your neck prickle with anticipation. You stare through the binoculars. There must be at least ten vehicles out there, all filled with bandits. The first has a red skull with silver teeth painted across the hood. The rest are behind it, hidden in the dust churned up by its wheels. As they get closer, their motors roar.

Suddenly, your slingshot seems flimsy, your bulletproof vest too thin.

The Land Rovers stop. The dust dies down.

"Slingshots ready," calls Duba. "Aim and—"

"Duba!" Bahar cries from along the wall. "Their tires are hidden."

Shocked, you realize she's right. Metal sheets are attached to the bandits' vehicles, shielding their tires from your darts.

"No," cries Duba. "We have to stop them from getting closer, or they'll attack us. Youngsters, get down from the wall to safety. Bahar, take everyone to the training hall."

There must be some way to stop those vehicles. Something you can do.

"This way. Fast." Bahar hustles you all down from the wall, across a courtyard, past the storage room for the school supplies. The door is ajar.

"That's it!" You cry. "Follow me."

Dashing into the storage room, you rip open boxes of balloons and paint. "Quick, pour the paint into balloons and tie a knot in the top. We'll paint bomb their windscreens so they can't drive any closer."

"Great idea," calls Tracey. "Come, Bahar and you others, help!"

With so many kids helping, you soon have a box of paint bombs. You, Tracey and Bahar race back to the top of the wall.

"Get back down," yells Duba. "I told you youngsters to stay away. It's getting too dangerous. I said—"

The roar of Land Rovers drowns out his voice. The bandits have nearly reached the compound.

Bahar ignores Duba. Crouching behind the raised outer edge of the wall, she tips the paint bombs onto the floor so you and Tracey can reach them.

You fire a paint bomb at the nearest Land Rover. It splatters over the windscreen, fluorescent pink paint dribbling down over the red skull on its hood. Yellow follows. Then green. Blinded by paint, the bandits grind to a halt.

"Good thinking," calls Duba.

Beside you, Tracey has covered another Land Rover in blue, gold and silver. Bahar has covered hers with green and brown, the colors merging so the windscreen looks like it's splattered with poo.

Turning, you aim more bombs at nearby vehicles. You're just about out of paint, when the bandits lunge out of the Land Rovers, holding wicked knives.

"Hide," Duba yells. "We've got this. Agh—"

His cry is cut off as a knife flashes past you, hitting him in the arm.

"Grab him Bahar!" You load. Fire at a bandit just outside the wall. Paint splatters over the bandit's face. Reloading, you fire another paint bomb.

The bandit screams, rubbing his eyes and flees back towards the vehicles. Another bandit races towards the wall, his knife raised. Reaching for a paint bomb, you fumble. There are none. They're all gone.

Out of the corner of your eye, you glimpse the blue paint-splattered Land Rover that Bahar hit, and have an idea.

Down in the courtyard, a woman is tending Duba's wound. Bahar is heading up the stairs to the wall with another box of paint bombs.

"Bahar," you call, "Tracey will grab those. Go and get sacks of camel dung as fast as you can."

Grabbing some youngsters to help her, Bahar dashes off.

Tracey plonks the carton of paint bombs down next to you. You both reload, fire, and spray more bandits with paint.

Soon, Bahar is passing large bags of camel dung along the wall to the guards and slingshot crew.

You pick up a ball of dung. It's smelly and warm. Even though the outside is firm, you can tell the inside isn't.

"Gross," says Tracey, going for paint bombs instead. "That stinks."

"That's the point."

A grappling hook flies up over the wall past the guards. The rope on the end pulls taut. You glance over the edge. A bandit with a huge scar on his cheek is making his way up the wall. You load your camel poop in the yellow tubing and line your laser up on Scar Cheek's face.

Scar Cheek bellows to his friends to join him. You fire. The dung hits him in the face, some of it entering his open mouth. Yowling, he spits, letting go of the rope, and falls to the desert below.

The rest of the slingshot crew leap to action, firing dung balls at more bandits. The old hard dung makes them yelp with pain. The fresher dung makes them bellow and curse.

Paintballs fly. Every bandit is covered in paint, poo or both. Some are chased by swarms of flies.

Scar Cheek shouts, signaling his men to retreat. You were so busy firing, you hadn't realized all the bandits had cleaned their Land Rovers' windscreens. Within a few minutes, only empty balloons, scattered camel poo, and abandoned ropes and weapons remain – and a cloud of red dust marking the bandits' retreat.

"Phew," says Tracey, wiping her paint-splattered hands on her even-more-paint-splattered armored vest.

Your own hands are covered in dung and you smell like a camel's rear end. "Oh well," you say, "someone had to get their hands dirty."

"I'm just glad it wasn't me," says Tracey. "Paint is bad enough. The dung was a great idea though."

"Yeah, it worked."

"It certainly did," says a deep voice.

You spin.

Duba's behind you, holding his bandaged arm against his body. "Excellent job. Everyone helped, but due to your great ideas, we got rid of those bandits. As soon as you've cleaned yourself up, Karim wants to see you." He wrinkles his nose. "Make sure you use lots of soap."

Everyone laughs.

Duba addresses the whole slingshot crew. "Well done, youngsters. Merchant Karim wants to reward you all for your hard work."

Reward? Could that mean…?

Tracey nudges you. "Come on, stinky, I'm dying for a shower."

It turns out, Karim doesn't have showers, only baths. You soak in a huge warm tub of bubbles, but not for long. You're keen to see what that reward is.

Once you're dried and dressed in clean clothes, you're dismayed at the dirty multi-colored ring you've left around the bath.

A maid bustles in. "Don't you worry about that. You're a hero today, so no cleaning for you. Go and see merchant Karim immediately."

Grinning, you race to the training area.

Tracey smiles. "You smell much better," she says, digging her elbow into your ribs.

Entering the hall, Karim shakes your hand vigorously and greets the slingshot crew and guards. "You have all shown great resourcefulness and resilience today. Those bandits are terrifying, but you faced them with bravery." He strides to the cabinet in the corner and presses an alarm pad on the wall, turning off the lasers.

Lifting the beautiful helmet from the stand, he brings it over and faces you. "Everyone was brave today, but you were brilliant, coming up with paint bombs and dung balls. Wear this helmet with pride when you return home."

"Thank you." You grin. "Um, did you say *return home?*"

"Yes, I'm sending you home." He places the helmet on your head.

Wow, you can hardly believe you won the helmet. It fits perfectly and makes you feel amazing. With a helmet like this, you don't need a new bike.

The merchant calls to a guard, "Saddle up Jamina.

They're ready to go home."

"How?" asks Tracey.

"Easy," he replies. "When Jamina jumps off the compound wall, a portal to your world will open."

"J-Jumps off the c-compound wall?" stutters Tracey.

"I'm sure that'll be simple for two adventurers like you." He laughs, winking at you.

Everyone cheers as you and Tracey climb up on Jamina. How she negotiates the narrow stone stairs up the compound wall is a mystery, but soon you're at the top.

"Ready?" she asks. Without waiting for an answer, she leaps.

In a brilliant flash of light, you're back on the trail at Mystic Portal.

Congratulations, you've ridden a camel and a magic carpet, defeated the desert bandits with your brilliant ideas and become a hero.

On every trail you bike, people admire your amazing helmet. You often return to Mystic Portal to have many more adventures.

You could ride a sea turtle, explore an underwater city, or go to a party with hundreds of furry orange creatures. Or you could continue your desert adventure by finding out what happens if you speak politely to the magic carpet.

It's time to make a decision. Do you:

Go back and talk to the magic carpet politely? **P36**

Go to the list of choices and start reading from another part of the story? **P248**

Or

Go back to the beginning a try another path? **P1**

Race Jamina in the Camel Races

"I'd love to race Jamina, you say, shaking Aamir's hand and smiling at Latifah, even though you're not looking forward to another bone rattling ride. "And thank you for your generous offer of accommodation. The desert is a harsh place so I'd be happy to stay with you."

You'd also be happy to go home, but you don't mention that. It'll probably upset him again.

In no time at all, you're in Aamir's tent, eating a delicious salad of couscous, juicy figs and oranges, and drinking cool fresh lake water from a water skin.

When you're finished, Aamir whisks you into another part of the tent and pulls a large red headscarf from a bag.

"Here, this will protect you from sand and dust," he says, wrapping the scarf around your head and over your nose, and securing it. "Red is my family's color. You honor us by wearing it."

Taking you outside, he checks Jamina's saddle is secure, and helps you up.

Holding Jamina's halter, Aamir leads you past a hubbub of people among the tents, and through date palms and orange trees – which account for today's lunch. Soon you're out on the track that surrounds the oasis. Camels and their riders are milling behind a rope held by two young children – an improvised start line.

There are ten camels in all, and a betting stand with a queue of people placing bets. The sidelines are crowded with spectators. The whole oasis must be here.

Flashing his teeth, Amir smiles up at you. "If you win today, I'll split the prize with you."

Prize? "That's generous of you, Amir. What's the prize?"

"Half a pound of gold. Good luck." He strolls off to the sidelines.

Half a pound of gold? Your mouth hangs open like an empty saddlebag as you think of all the things you could do with gold. You could even buy new bikes for you and Sidney, just as good as Tracey's – if you ever get home again. Now the race seems like a much better idea.

"Are you ready?" asks Jamina, striding over to stand behind the starting rope.

"Sure, any time."

An official strolls along the row of camels, inspecting them and prodding the jockeys. He finds a leather pouch under one jockey's saddle and opens it, sprinkling a pinch of yellow powder on the ground. In a guttural voice, he sends the jockey and camel off the racecourse.

"Why aren't they racing?" you ask Jamina.

"That's a saffron bomb. It makes camels sneeze and their eyes water. Saffron bombs are banned, so that rider's disqualified."

The official prods a young rider's ribs and sends his

camel away too.

"Some families starve their jockeys to make them lighter so they can win the race," says Jamina. "They're also disqualified."

At the far end of the line, the official yells and two camels are dispatched from the racecourse.

"What was that about?"

Through her solid body, Jamina's camel chuckle makes her sides thrum and tickles your legs. "Those two have hidden small rockets under their saddles. They get out in front, and explode the rockets, making their camels run faster and the ones behind run away in fear." Jamina snorts. "Some camels are sillier than others. I'm not spooked by a stupid rocket."

With four camels disqualified, there are only six left – Jamina and five others. "Do you think we have a chance of winning?" you ask.

"More chance than those cheats," replies Jamina, snorting again.

You really must talk to her about snorting so much.

The crowd quiets. Aamir gives you the thumbs up and winks.

A man in gleaming white raises his arm, and then drops it. The children let go of the rope.

With thundering hooves, camels race off, dust rising around you. You wish you had your sunglasses on, rather than in your backpack in Aamir's tent. Your body lurches wildly from side to side. You try to move in time with her as Jamina speeds up.

The rider on the camel to your left whips his camel. It cuts in front of you, blocking off Jamina's path. With one of her infamous snorts, Jamina nips the other camel's flank. It veers off the race course. You and Jamina spurt forward through the gap.

All the other riders have whips. They beat their camels, and surge forward, leaving you and Jamina to eat their dust.

Even if you had a whip, you wouldn't want to use it on Jamina. She's been your friend and saved your life. You mentally kiss the gold goodbye. It was a nice dream, but there's no way you're going to catch up with those other camels now. You can't even see them, the cloud of dust is so thick. Glad for the headscarf over your mouth, you hunker down on Jamina's back. The dust seems thicker. The camels' hooves, louder.

Through the haze, camels appear. You're gaining on them. You pass one and pat Jamina's side. "Well done, girl."

The dust starts to clear. Palms on the side of the track peek above the dust cloud. There are only three camels in front of you. Wow, you may have a chance of winning after all. But as you pass the camel on your right, the rider flings something. A billowing cloud of yellow fills the air – a saffron bomb. The official must have missed one. Water streams from your stinging eyes as Jamina runs straight through the yellow haze, snorting and bellowing. Ahead, an inhuman shriek of pain fills the air. One of the camels has stumbled. It lies on the ground, its hind legs splayed right in your path. Jamina will never be able to stop in time. You're going to crash. Your race will be over.

Jamina charges. Leaps. And clears the camel's legs.

"Yahoo! Go girl," you shriek at the top of your voice.

Another snort. Jamina's hooves thunder along the compacted sand, chasing the lone camel. Not far now. Nearly there.

The leading rider glances back, shooting you a panicked look. She reaches under her saddle and pulls out a roll of something. A blanket? How is that going to help her? She flings the blanket in front of her and it unfurls hovering just above the race track.

Not a blanket! A flying carpet. The camel jumps on board, rider and all. They take off, zooming along the track, just above the sand.

There are no spectators here. Palm trees and bushes around the oasis shield this pair of cheaters from being spotted.

"Not fair," you yell, although it's no use. You'll never win now. Oh, well, at least the thought of gold was nice for a while.

You're tossed from side to side as Jamina bolts along

the track.

"Slow down, girl. We're never going to win."

Ignoring you, she charges ahead, kicking up dust behind you.

Yeah, she's right. If you're going to race, you may as well finish. Palm trees blur as Jamina races past them. Something flashes among the palms, but you've no time to look, because the carpet in front is slowing.

"Come on, Jamina. Let's race!" You slap your hand against your thigh.

Jamina spurts ahead. She wasn't joking when she said camels could run 40 miles an hour. Her speed is brutal, but your butt will never be the same again.

Through the palms, you catch a glimpse of the lake, and beyond it, colorful tents. "Come on, girl, we're nearly at the finish line."

Giving one last spurt of speed, Jamina shoots ahead, narrowing the gap between you and the cheaters on the magic carpet.

Abruptly, the carpet stops. The camel steps off.

Jamina races forward. She's nearly caught up to them.

The cheater's camel lashes out with its hind legs. A thud ricochets through Jamina's body.

"Mwoooaaaah!" Her shriek of pain knifes through you. She lurches. Staggers. Nearly throws you off.

"Jamina, are you okay?"

Her breathing is labored, heavy, but she keeps going,

staggering forward at a half run, around the corner.

In the distance, the cheaters cross the finish line. Spectators roar.

Behind you, around the bend, telltale dust rises in the air. The other camels are closing the gap, catching up. Still, Jamina staggers forward, running unevenly.

Patting her flank, you encourage her. "You're doing well, girl. We're nearly there."

You glance behind to check your competitors. What are those dark splotches in the red sand? Deep-crimson splotches. Jamina's blood!

She's been so faithful, run so well, and saved your life in the desert. It's so unfair. "Jamina, you're hurt." Tears well in your eyes. "You don't have to finish. You've run well."

No answer. How you wish she'd snort, chuckle, or say something. The only sounds are her harsh breathing, the uneven thuds of her hooves, and the drumming hoofbeats behind you, getting ever closer.

The finish line looms. The crowd becomes distinct faces. Worried and anxious, you ignore the spectators, rubbing Jamina's neck as she slows, plodding across the finish line.

A moment later, the other camels catch up and race past you, leaving you and Jamina standing in the middle of the track, eating their dust.

The crowd cheers.

Don't they realize your camel's hurt?

She bends her front legs, kneeling. You're off her back before her rear haunches sink to the ground. Racing around to her head, you inspect her for damage.

A gash in her chest is bleeding. You rip your headscarf off and use it to staunch the blood.

Aamir rushes to your side. "How did she hurt herself?"

"She didn't. The rider in front of us cheated, and then that camel hurt her."

"Looks like a gash from a hoof," Amir announces. Before you can explain any further, he signals some men to take care of Jamina, and a loud horn blows.

The rest of the racing camels gather back near the finish line.

"They're announcing the results," Aamir says.

The official strides over to the cheater whose camel gashed Jamina and holds the rider's hand high in the air. They both beam as the official calls out something in Arabic.

You're about to protest, when the crowd parts and man strides forward, a camera with an enormous telescopic lens hanging around his neck. Yelling at the official, he grabs the camera and points to the screen.

The official steps over to take a look. Sidling closer, you peer over the man's shoulder. The photo clearly shows the cheater and camel using a flying carpet to win the race. That flash in the palms as you were racing, must have been from his camera.

Shouting, the official waves his arms in the air like an agitated windmill. Two men run over and drag the rider away.

Aamir approaches you. "They're disqualified. That means we won the race." His white teeth gleam against his dark beard in an enormous grin. "Well done."

Within moments, you're hoisted on people's shoulders. The crowd cheers. People stomp and whistle. Somewhere, a loud horn is blown.

You look for Jamina, but she's gone.

"It's alright," says Aamir, when he sees you searching. "My best healers are taking care of her. Soon she'll be well enough to do the victory lap with you."

Victory lap? There's no way she can run, but you nod, too tired to argue. When will you ever get home again? And where are Tracey and Sidney?

In the evening, as you're nestled in the sand next to Jamina, leaning against her side, Aamir approaches. "You raced well today," he says. "You must have a lot of racing experience."

Thinking of all the bike tracks you've been on with Tracey and Sidney, you smile. "I have done some racing, but not on camelback. The credit really goes to Jamina."

Jamina raises her head and snorts. A good sign, she must be feeling better.

Aamir peels back the bandage on her chest. Taking a small clay pot from his robe, he smears smelly salve over Jamina's wound. Grinning, he replaces the bandage. "This salve will do wonders," he says. "You should both be able to do your victory lap by tomorrow."

No way, she'll need longer to heal, but you don't say it out loud.

Aamir gives you a blanket. "I'm guessing you'd rather sleep out here, under the stars by Jamina."

"You're right." Your eyes grow heavy and you fall asleep to the sound of his footsteps traipsing away through the sand.

Someone shakes you awake. You squint in the bright morning sun.

Aamir is bending over you. "Let's check Jamina's wound."

When he rips off the bandage, you're astounded. "How's that possible? Her wound's gone!" You rub Jamina's smooth fur, amazed that the gash has healed.

Aamir hands you your backpack, an orange and some figs. "I've put some wonder salve in your backpack," he says, "just in case you need it one day. You looked tired, so I let you sleep late, but now you must eat. The victory lap is in a few minutes."

The orange is juicy and the figs are sweet – a breakfast for royalty. Aamir saddles up Jamina while you're eating and soon you're astride her, heading for the race course.

"Wow, I didn't expect this. There are nearly as many folk as yesterday." They start cheering as you approach.

Jamina snorts. "Of course there are," she says. "We're important, we won the race."

"So now we race again?" you ask.

Another snort tells you you're wrong. "Of course not," Jamina replies, stepping on to the track.

An official stands before you with two bulging leather pouches. He passes one to Aamir and the other to you. The gold. Wow. Hastily, you stuff yours in your backpack as Jamina walks along the track. The crowd's clapping and cheering nearly deafens you. People throw handfuls of leaves and flower petals towards you, like confetti swirling through the air. As Jamina walks, she turns her head to gaze at the crowd. Her eyelashes flutter, and her lips are pulled off her teeth in a weird camel smile. She looks like a queen greeting her subjects.

You smother a chuckle.

A short distance along the track, two children hold a rope.

"We only go that far?" you ask Jamina.

She nods. "Thank you for being such a loyal rider. I have a special gift for you."

"There's no need for a gift," you say. "You saved my life in the desert and I've had a wonderful time with you. That's enough."

Instead of snorting, Jamina turns her long neck

towards you. Did she just wink?

The crowd is still cheering from the sidelines as you cross the finish line.

With a flash, Jamina and the desert disappear. You're back on your bike, trees zipping past you, as you burst out of the forest into the sand dunes at the bottom of Mystic Portal. Crashing breakers on the beach below tell you that you're at the end of the bike trail.

Bracing yourself for the shock of your tires sliding on sand, you gasp when your bike whizzes through the sand smoothly. How is it possible? You glance down. The rims of your wheels are wider and you have enormous fat tires, especially made for traversing sand. Laughing, you realize the fat sand tires are Jamina's gift. They remind you of her wide feet tromping through the desert. At the top of the dune, you launch your bike into the air and as you land, small puffs of sand rise around your tires. You could swear you heard a camel snort.

A whoop sounds behind you and Tracey and Sidney break out of the tree line, heading over the dunes towards you. Thinking of the gold in your backpack, and all the great biking gear you can buy for you and your friends, you grin and call out, "Hey, have I got something to tell you two!"

Congratulations, you've had a successful adventure on Mystic Portal. With all the gold you've earned racing camels, you buy new bikes for Tracey, Sidney and yourself and set up a mountain biking charity to help kids who can't afford bikes. Every now and then, you jump over Camel Hump to visit Jamina for old times' sake. There are many more adventures on Mystic Portal. Maybe you'd like to tour the underwater city of Hydropolis, tame an ogre, discover the mysterious track builders or ride a seahorse.

It's time to make a decision. Do you:

Go back and ride with Tracey on the tatty flying carpet? **P24**

Go to the list of choices and start reading from another part of the story? **P248**

Or

Go back to the beginning a try another path? **P1**

Go to the library and read

"Some quiet time would be great." You climb off Sharmeena's back. "I'd love to read for a while, then come to the party after."

A soft glow shines from the left passage.

"It's only short way to the library," says Sharmeena. "When you're done, I'll bring you to the party."

"Thanks, I'd love that. What about you, Sidney?"

"I'll stick with you."

"I'll gather everyone for your party. See you soon." Sharmeena bounds down the tunnel.

A few moments later, you and Sidney enter the library. It's rather small, with a single shelf of books that all look similar.

Sidney settles onto a large cushion and falls asleep. He must be worn out after his ordeal with Bog.

A track-keeper gestures to the shelf. "Read as long as you like, and call me if you need anything."

Wandering over to the shelf, you investigate the contents. All the books are You Say Which Way adventures.

Sidney's sleeping peacefully, so you start to read, knowing that at any time you can stop and go to the party. The strangest thing is that every book is a preview, only one chapter long. Soon you're racing through the books, enjoying yourself.

Free Previews

Preview: Dragons Realm

"Hey, Fart-face!"

Uh oh. The Thompson twins are lounging against a fence as you leave the corner store – Bart, Becks, and Bax. They're actually the Thomson triplets, but they're not so good at counting, so they call themselves twins. Nobody has dared tell them different.

They stare at you. Bart, big as an ox. Becks, smaller but meaner. And Bax, the muscle. As if they need it.

Bart grins like an actor in a toothpaste commercial. "What have you got?" He swaggers towards you.

Becks sneers, stepping out with Bax close behind. "Come on, squirt, hand it over," she calls, her meaty hands bunching into fists.

Your backpack is heavy with goodies. Ten chocolate bars and two cans of tuna fish for five bucks – how could you resist? And now you could lose it all. The twins form a human wall, blocking the sidewalk. There's no way around them.

Seriously? All this fuss over chocolate? Not again! They've been bullying you and your friends for way too long. There's still time to outsmart them before the bus leaves for the school picnic.

A girl walks between you and the twins. You make

your move, sprinting off towards the park next to school. Your backpack is heavy, but you've gained a head start on those numb skulls.

Becks roars.

"Charge," yells Bax,

"Get the snot-head," Bart bellows. Their feet pound behind you as you make it around the corner through the park gate. Now to find a hiding place.

On your right is a thick grove of trees. They'll never find you in there, not without missing the bus to the picnic.

To your left, is a sports field. Behind the bleachers, there's a hole in the fence. If you can make it through that hole, you're safe. They're much too big to follow.

Their pounding footsteps are getting closer. They'll be around the corner soon.

It is time to make a decision. Do you:

Race across the park to the hole in the fence?

Or

Hide from the Thompson twins in the trees?

To keep reading previews, turn the page. **P222**
Or
You can go to the track-keepers' party. **P79**

Preview: Deadline Delivery

Out of breath from climbing stairs, you finally reach Level 8 of Ivory Tower. Down the hallway, past a tattoo parlor, Deadline Delivery's neon sign glows red. The word Dead flickers as you approach.

It's two minutes past seven in the morning – is Deadline Delivery's dispatch office open yet? Yes, through the mesh-covered window in the steel door, Miss Betty is slouched behind her cluttered desk. You knock and smile as if you want to be here.

Miss Betty turns and scowls at you. Nothing personal – she scowls at everyone. She presses a button and the steel door squeaks and squeals open.

"Good morning, ma'am. Got any work for me today?" you ask.

She sighs, scratches her left armpit, and taps at her computer. Then she rummages through a long shelf of packages and hands you a plastic-wrapped box and two grimy dollar coins. "Urgent delivery," she says. "Pays ten bucks, plus toll fees."

Ten dollars is more than usual. Suspicious, you check the box's delivery label. "390 Brine Street? That's in the middle of pirate territory!"

She shrugs. "If you're too scared, there are plenty of other kids who'll do it."

Scared? You're terrified. But you both know she's right

– if you don't take this job, someone else will. And you really need the money – you have exactly three dollars in the whole world, and your last meal was lunch yesterday. "Thank you, Miss Betty."

"Uniform," she says, pointing to the box of Deadline Delivery caps.

You pick up the least dirty cap. What's that stink? Has something died in it? You swap it for the second-least dirty one and put that on. You'd rather not wear any kind of uniform – sometimes it's better to not attract attention in public – but Miss Betty insists.

The steel door squeaks and starts to close, and you hurry out. Miss Betty doesn't say goodbye. She never does.

After stashing the package in your backpack and the toll coins in your pocket, you hurry down the stairs to the food court on Level 5. Time to grab a quick breakfast. This might be your last meal ever, and there's no sense in dying hungry. This early in the morning, only Deep-Fried Stuff and Mac's Greasy Spoon are open, so there's not a lot of choice.

In Mac's Greasy Spoon, Mac himself cuts you a nice thick slice of meatloaf for a dollar, and you smile and thank him, even though his meatloaf is always terrible.

If there's any meat in it, you don't want to know what kind. At least it's cheap and filling. After a few bites, you wrap the rest in a plastic bag and put it in your pocket for lunch.

You walk back down the stairs to Ivory Tower's main entrance on Level 3. Levels 1 and 2 are somewhere further down, underwater, but you've never seen them. The polar ice caps melted and flooded the city before you were born.

From beside the bulletproof glass doors, a bored-looking guard looks up. "It's been quiet out there so far this morning," she tells you, as she checks a security camera screen. "But there was pirate trouble a few blocks north of the Wall last night. And those wild dogs are roaming around again too. Be careful, kid."

The doors grind open, just a crack, enough for you to squeeze through and out onto Nori Road. Well, everyone calls it a road, although the actual road surface is twenty feet under the murky water.

Both sides of the so-called road have sidewalks of rusty girders and planks and bricks and other junk, bolted or welded or nailed to the buildings – none of it's too safe to walk on, but you know your way around.

Just below the worn steel plate at your feet, the water's calm. Everything looks quiet. No boats in sight. A few people are fishing out their windows. Fish for breakfast? Probably better than meatloaf.

Far over your head, a mag-lev train hums past on a rail bridge. Brine Street's only a few minutes away by train – for rich people living up in the over-city. Not you.

Mac once told you that most over-city people never leave the sunny upper levels, and some of them don't even don't know the city's streets are flooded down here. Or don't care, anyway. Maybe that's why there are so many security fences between up there and down here, so that over-city people can pretend that under-city people like you don't exist.

There are fences down here too. To your left, in the distance, is Big Pig's Wall – a heavy steel mesh fence, decorated with spikes and barbed wire and the occasional skeleton. The same Wall surrounds you in every direction, blocking access above and below the waterline – and Brine Street's on the other side. The extra-dangerous side.

Big Pig's Wall wasn't built to keep people in – no, it's to keep pirates out.

The heavily guarded Tollgates are the only way in or out, and to go through them, everyone has to pay a toll to Big Pig's guards. A dollar per person, more for boats, all paid into big steel-bound boxes marked Donations. Big Pig has grown rich on those "donations". Not as rich as over-city people, but still richer than anyone else in this neighborhood. Some people grumble that Big Pig and his guards are really no better than the pirate gangs, but most locals think the tolls are a small price to pay for some peace and security.

Then again, you happen to know the Tollgates *aren't*

the only way in and out – last week, you found a secret tunnel that leads through the Wall. No toll fees if you go that way – two dollars saved. You finger the coins in your pocket.

It's time to make a decision.

How will you get to Brine Street? Do you:

Go the longer and safer route through a Tollgate?

Or

Save time and money, and try the secret tunnel?

To keep reading previews, turn the page. **P227**

Or

You can go to the track-keepers' party. **P79**

Preview: Between the Stars.

In a sleep tank on the space ship *Victoria*, your dreaming cap teaches you as you float.

You first put on a dreaming cap for the space sleep test. Although you thought it looked like you had an octopus on your head, you didn't joke about it. Nobody did. Everyone wanted to pass the test and go to the stars.

Passing meant a chance to get out of overcrowded Londinium.

If you didn't pass, you'd likely be sent to a prison factory in Northern Europa. Nobody wanted to go there, even though Britannica hasn't been a good place lately, Europa was said to be worse.

When the judge sentenced you to transportation for stealing that food, you sighed inside with relief. You knew transportation was the chance of a better life on a faraway planet, but only if you passed the sleep test.

You lined up with other hopefuls and waded into a pool of warm sleep jelly. They were all young, like you, and they all looked determined.

"Stay calm," the robot instructed. "Breathe in slowly through your mouthpiece and relax."

Nearby, a young woman struggled from the pool. She pulled out her breathing plug and gasped for breath.

"Take her back," said a guard. You knew what that meant – back to prison and then the factories. A convict sneered at the poor girl, the cruel look on his face magnified by a scar running down one cheek.

In your short time in prison, you had learned there were people who would have been criminals no matter what life they'd been born to. Something told you that he was one of them.

You put him out of your mind and concentrated on doing what the robot said. You thought of the warm porridge you'd had every morning in the orphanage growing up. The sleeping jelly didn't seem so strange then. When your head was submerged, you breathed in slowly.

As the jelly filled your lungs, you fought against thoughts of drowning. You'd listened at the demonstration and knew it was oxygenated. *This must be what it's like to be a fish*, you'd thought as you moved forward through the thick fluid, *I only have to walk through to the other side.*

Closing your eyes, you moved forward through the thick warm jelly. "Relax," you told yourself. "You can do this."

You opened your eyes just in time to see the scar-faced youth about to knock your breather off. Thankfully, the jelly slowed his punch and you ducked out of the way just in time.

Then, a moment later, you were on the other side being handed a towel.

"This one's a yes," intoned a man in a white coat. He slapped a bracelet on your wrist and sent you down a corridor away from your old life. As you exited, you just had time to hear the fate of the scar-faced youth. "He'll do. Take him to the special room."

Days of training followed. You often joined other groups of third class passengers but you didn't see Scar-Face among them.

You passed all the tests and then one day, you got into a sleep tank beside hundreds of others. Your dreaming cap would teach you everything you'd need to know in your new life.

You were asleep when the *Victoria* was launched into space. You slept as the *Victoria* lost sight of the Earth and then its star, the sun.

And here you are, years later, floating in sleep fluid and learning with your dreaming cap. Or you were. Because now you hear music.

Oxygen hisses into your sleeping chamber and the fluid you have been immersed in starts to drain away. Next time you surface, you'll breathe real air, something that your lungs haven't done in a long time.

"Sleeper one two seven six do you accept this mission? Sleeper, please engage if you wish to awaken for this mission. Sleeper, there are other suitable travelers for this mission. Do you choose to wake?"

Passengers can sleep the entire journey if they want.

They can arrive at the new planet without getting any older. First class passengers will own land and riches when they arrive but you're third class, you have nothing.

Groggily, you listen to the voice. If you choose to take on a mission, you can earn credit for the new planet – even freedom – but you could also arrive on the new planet too old to use your freedom.

"Sleeper, do you accept the mission?"

It is time to make your first decision.

Do you want to wake up and undertake this mission?

Or

Do you wait for a different mission or wait to land on the new planet?

To keep reading previews, turn the page. **P231**
Or
You can go to the track-keepers' party. **P79**

Preview: Dinosaur Canyon

A meteorite streaks across a cloudless Montana sky and disappears behind a hill, not far away.

"Anyone see that?" you say to your classmates as you point towards the horizon.

Around the bus, a couple of students look up from their phones. "What? Huh?"

"The meteorite. Did you see it?"

"Meteor what?" the kid sitting next to you asks.

"Never mind." You shake your head and wonder if you're the only one who's really interested in this fieldtrip.

"I saw it," Paulie Smith says from a seat near the back. "That was amazing!"

As you and Paulie search the sky for more meteorites, the bus turns off the main road and passes an old wooden sign.

WELCOME TO GABRIEL'S GULCH.

"Right," Mister Jackson says, as the bus comes to a stop. "Once your tents are set up, you've got the afternoon to go exploring. So get to it. And remember, take notes on what you see and hear. You *will* be tested."

You're hoping to find some fossils. You might even get lucky and stumble across a piece of that meteorite. That would be awesome.

After locating a level patch of ground near a clump of

saltbush, you set up your dome tent and toss your sleeping bag and air mattress inside with the rest of your gear. Then you grab your daypack and water bottle. You'd never think of going for a hike without taking water with you. They don't call this area the *Badlands* without good reason.

A couple of energy bars, an apple, compass, box of matches, waterproof flashlight, folding army shovel and some warm clothing go into your daypack as well, just in case.

Mister Jackson is drinking coffee with some parents who've come along to help. They've set up the kitchen near the junction of a couple of old stone walls as protection from the wind and are laughing and telling tales of other camping trips.

"My tent's up Mister J, so I'm off to look around."

He nods. "Make sure you fill in the logbook with your intentions. Oh, and who're you teaming up with? Remember our talk on safety – you're not allowed to go wandering about alone. And watch out for rattlesnakes."

You look at the chaos around camp. Rather than being interested in dinosaur fossils, which is the main reason for this trip, most of your fellow students are puzzling over how their borrowed tents work or complaining about the cell phone reception. Camping equipment is strewn everywhere. Apart from you, Paulie is the only one who's managed to get his tent up so far.

"Hey, Paulie. I'm heading out. Want to tag along?"

Paulie points to his chest. "Who? Me?"

Paulie's not really a friend. He's a year behind you at school, but at least he seems interested in being here. He's even got a flag with a picture of a T. Rex working at the front counter of a burger joint, flying over his tent. Chuckling, you ponder the silliness of a short-armed dinosaur flipping burgers

"Yeah, you, get a move on." You walk over and write in the camp's log book. *Going west towards hills with Paulie. Back in time for dinner.*

"What are we going to do?" Paulie asks.

"Explore those hills," you say, pointing off into the west. "Quick, grab your pack and let's go ... before Mr. J or one of the parents decide to come along."

As Paulie shoves a few supplies in his bag, you look across the scrubland towards the badly-eroded hills in the distance. It's ideal country for finding fossils. Erosion is the fossil hunter's best friend. Who knows what the recent rains have uncovered for a sharp-eyed collector like yourself.

"Did you know they've found Tyrannosaurus Rex bones around here?" Paulie says as the two of you head out of camp.

You pull the *Pocket Guide to the Montana Badlands* out of your back pocket and hold it up. "I've been reading up too."

"But did you know scientists reckon T. Rex had arms about the same length as man's but would have been strong enough to bench press over 400 pounds?"

"Yeah?" you say, remembering Paulie's love of obscure facts and how he drives everyone at school crazy with them. "Well according to this book, there's been more dinosaur fossils found in Montana than anywhere else in the country."

Paulie nods. "I want to find an Ankylosaurus. They're built like a tank with armor and everything. They had horns sticking out of the sides of their heads and a mean looking club on the end of their tails!"

That would be pretty awesome. "A tank eh? Maybe we'll find one of its scales embedded in the rock, or a horn sticking out of a cliff. Anything's possible when fossil hunting, that's what makes it so exciting."

You both stride off across the prairie with big smiles and high hopes. Fifteen minutes later, when you look back, the camp is nothing but a cluster of dots barely visible through the sagebrush.

"Where to from here?" Paulie asks.

"There's a couple of options. We could search for that meteorite. It must have come down somewhere around here."

"Maybe it landed in that canyon?" Paulie says, indicating a gap between two hills. "Could be all sorts of neat stuff in there."

"That's Gabriel's Gulch," you say, referring to the map in your guide. "Or we could look for fossils in those hills," you say, pointing to your right. "According to the guide, there's an abandoned mine over there too."

Your adventure is about to begin. It is time to make your first decision. Do you:

Go left into Gabriel's Gulch?

Or

Go right towards the eroded hills?

Wow, you've finished the previews of all the books in the track-keepers' library. That was fast.

As you close the last cover, Sidney stretches and yawns. "Hey, I've had a good sleep. Are you done reading yet?"

"Yeah, I'm done. These books are great, but they're only previews. I can't wait to read them, especially *Dragons Realm*."

"What other books are there?" asks Sidney.

"You'd love *Dinosaur Canyon* or the space travel one, *Between the Stars*. I bet Tracey would like *Deadline Delivery*, because it seems dangerous, but right now, I'm ready for the party."

"Yeah, me too. Let's get there before it starts." Sidney stands up.

Sharmeena comes through the door. "Ready?"

You nod.

"Good, hop on my back and we'll get going."

You and Sidney climb on Sharmeena's back and go to the party. **P183**

General Glossary

Asian Camels

Asian camels are known as Bactrian camels, and have two humps. These camels have high tolerance to cold, drought and high altitudes. In 2002 the population was estimated at only 800 camels, so now they are listed as a critically endangered species. A small number of these camels are found in Australia, although most Australian camels are dromedaries. (See dromedary below).

Camel eyelashes, eyebrows and nostrils

Camels have a double row of eyelashes to prevent sand entering their eyes. They also have prominent bony ridges above their eyes, which also helps shield their eyes from sand. Their large bushy eyebrows stop glare from the sun, and their nostrils can shut against sand.

Camel Feet

Camel feet are large and wide, which helps them walk on sand more easily. Camels have two toes on each foot. These are joined by webbing underneath the foot which allows the toes to spread as they walk on sand. The pads of their feet are covered with thick protective soles, and near the heel, camels have a ball of fat which cushions them as they walk.

Camel's Gait

A camel's gait, or the way it walks, is unusual. Camels and giraffes have long legs, short bodies, and large feet, so they walk in a similar manner. Camels and giraffes move both legs on the same side of their body at the same time.

Most four-legged animals move a foreleg (front leg) then the back leg (hind leg) on the opposite side of their body. For example, a horse walks like this: Right foreleg, then left hind leg, then right foreleg then left hind leg then right foreleg etc. RF, LH, LF, RH, repeated....

(Shorthand: RF=right foreleg; LF=left foreleg; RH=right hind leg; LH=left hind leg).

Camels walk with two legs at once on the same side: Right foreleg and right hind leg, then left foreleg and left hind leg etc. RF & RH, LF & LH, repeated....

A common explanation for the camel and giraffe's unusual gait is that this way of walking prevents their fore and hind feet from bumping – which would be a problem if they walked the way other animals walk, because their legs are so long.

Camel Hump is a Storage Cupboard

A camel's hump stores up to 80 pounds (36 kilograms) of fat. The camel breaks this down into water and energy when food and water are not available. These humps mean camels can travel up to 100 desert miles (161 kilometers) without water. A camel can go a week or more without water, and several months without food. They can drink up to 32 gallons (46 liters) of water at one drinking session! Camel's humps are quite firm to touch.

Unlike most mammals, a healthy camel's body temperature changes throughout the day from 93°F-107°F (34°C to 41.7°C). This allows the camel to conserve water by not sweating as the air temperature rises.

Camel Races

Camel races are often held in Arab countries and large amounts of money can be won when betting on camels. Recently, laws were made to outlaw child-jockeys (riders) in camel racing, because people were starving child-jockeys to make them lighter so their camels could win. No one starves their jockeys in Mystic Portal and all riders treat their camels with the love and care they deserve.

Dromedaries

The dromedary is a species of camel found in Arabia. Dromedaries have one hump. Fully-grown males weigh 880–1,320 lb (300–600kg), while females weigh 660–1,190 lb (300–540 kg). Camels have a long curved neck, a narrow chest and are covered in long, usually brown, hair. Camels are well-known for their tolerance to heat and for carrying burdens and riders across the desert.

Camels are herbivores – they eat desert vegetation, such as grasses, herbs, and leaves.

Hippocampus
Seahorse is the name given to 54 species of small marine fish, also known as Hippocampus. "Hippocampus" comes from the Ancient Greek word *hippos* meaning "horse" and *kampos* meaning "sea monster."

Male seahorses carry their eggs
Male seahorses carry their young after the female inserts mature eggs into a pouch on the male's belly.

Turtle Group
A group of turtles is known as a bale, nest, turn or a dole of turtles.

Mountain Biking Glossary

Mountain Biking (MTB)

Mountain bikes are bicycles that are used off roads, over rugged terrain. Mountain bike and mountain biking are often abbreviated as MTB in mountain biking communities. There are various styles of mountain bike riding. Specialized bikes are often used for each style. Some common biking categories are: cross country, Enduro, downhill, slalom, freeride, dirt jump, trials, street, marathon and trail riding. Definitions of these styles and some other mountain biking terms are below.

Air – Air describes how high you get off the ground when you take a jump. "Hey, I just got nine feet of air." "Did you get any air?" "How much air did you get?"

Air time – How long a bike is in the air after a jump. "I just had two seconds air time."

Berm – A built-up wall of dirt at the corner of a trail, or an embankment on a trail, or banked corner.

Boulder Garden/ Rock Garden – A section of the trail which is covered with big boulders that the rider needs to jump or bike over.

Chicken Line – A chicken line is a part of the trail that gives a rider the chance to go around a jump or an obstacle, instead of doing the jump, i.e.: an alternate less-risky route.

Cross Country (XC) – Riding from a start point to a destination (or in a loop) over various types of terrain. Cross country riding usually includes climbs and descents.

Directional Jump – In a directional jump, the rider has to change direction in midair before landing.

Dirt Jumping (DJ)/Dirt Jump Bike – Dirt jumpers ride bikes over shaped mounds of dirt (take-off ramps) to become airborne. They land on the landing ramp – usually another mound of dirt, some distance away. Some dirt jumps are designed to propel the biker high in the air. Others are designed to see how far the rider can get. Dirt jump bikes are simpler, with less moving parts (no gears etc), so they break less easily upon landing (or crashing).

Downhill / Downhill Trail / Downhill Ride (DH) – Mountain biking downhill on steep, rough terrain with obstacles such as jumps, drops or rock gardens. The fastest rider to the bottom wins. Downhill riding is often done on ski slopes or other steep areas, where riders get back to the top by ski tow, cable car or bus. Downhill riders have a reputation for speed and, sometimes, recklessness.

Downhill Jump – A bike jump designed so the take off point is higher than (or uphill from) the landing point.

Downhill Gap Jump – The take-off point is uphill from the landing point and there is a huge gap between both. See Gap Jump below.

Drop Jump / Drop / Drop Off – A ledge you can ride over. The rider drops off the ledge onto the trail below.

Dropping In – Dropping in is entering a steep track when other riders are around.

Dualie – A bike that has both front and rear suspension, i.e.: dual suspension. Suspension is a mechanical system that cushions the rider from hard landings and jolts, so a dualie is most comfortable to ride.

Endo – A crash when you fly over your handlebars, i.e.: over the end of your bike.

Enduro / All Mountain – A riding style similar to the type of racing in the Enduro World Series. This includes uphill climbs and downhill racing over technically challenging terrain. Enduro rides can take a whole day to complete.

Freeride / Big Hit / Hucking – Freeride is a do-anything style of riding that includes downhill racing, enormous jumps and skinny elevated bridges. It also includes stunts that require skill and aggression. Many of the most popular mountain bike videos online are freeriding.

Four Cross / Slalom (4X) – Riders compete on separate tracks, or on a short slalom track, with dirt jumps, berms and gap jumps.

Gap Jump – A gap jump has a take off ramp and a landing ramp, which are separated by a huge space in between. The most common example is a jump made of two dirt mounds with a pit or flat area between them. The aim of a gap jump is to be able to clear the distance easily. Failing to clear the gap often means smashing into reinforced timber at the front of the landing ramp.

Granny Gear – The lowest gear available on a bike, which only a grandmother would need to use. Designed for steep uphill climbing, but extremely easy to pedal in on flat ground.

Gravity Check – A fall.

Grinder – A long uphill climb.

Gutter Bunny – Someone who only bikes on the road – to school or work.

Hard-tail – A mountain bike that has no rear suspension – less comfortable to ride than a bike with full suspension. Suspension is a mechanical system that cushions the rider from hard landings and jolts.

Lid – Helmet.

Marathon/Touring – Long distance riding on dirt roads or a long single track. This includes mixed-terrain touring, which is riding over many types of surfaces on a single track with a bike suited for all types of surface.

Nose Wheelie – A reverse wheelie riding technique. The rider elevates the rear wheel while still rolling on the front tire.

Shred – Riding trails with speed and skill so other riders are impressed.

Skinny – A narrow bridge, sometimes high above the ground, which bikers ride along.

Step Up – A jump, with a gap, that takes you to a higher level. You jump your bike up over a step to the next level up a slope. Many bikers say step ups are the ultimate thrill, so these are often placed at the end of a trail, so the ride ends with a great jump.

Street Riding / Urban – Riders perform tricks by riding on (or over) man-made objects.

Switchback – A sharp corner on a trail, like the corners in a zigzag. Usually switchbacks help you climb hills that are too steep to pedal straight up.

Tabletop Jumps – This kind of jump has a flat platform connecting the on-ramp and off-ramp. Less experienced riders can land on the tabletop (platform), but more experienced riders will clear the entire jump and land on the off-ramp. Some people believe that table-tops are less risky than gaps because there is no gap to clear. But all jumps are dangerous. Table-tops look easier than gap jumps, so less-skilled riders may be tempted to try table-tops that are beyond their ability.

Trackstand – A riding technique: when the rider stops without putting a foot down.

Trail riding – Riding trails, such as unpaved tracks, forest paths, and signposted routes in recreational reserves. Trails can be a single track or a group of trails that form a trail center. (Don't confuse this with Trials riding).

Trials – Trial riders hop and jump bikes over obstacles, without touching their feet on the ground. Trials riding can be off-road or in town. Street-trials riders use man-made structures in a city or town. (Don't confuse this with Trail riding).

Wipeout – Crash. An old surfing term, used by bikers.

Wheelie – Lifting the front wheel off the ground, usually done by pulling on the handlebars, pedaling harder, and balancing well.

Wheelie Drop – A combination of a wheelie and a jump. Riders use wheelie drops to jump off a ledge at low speed when they only have a short run-up.

Whoop-De-Dos – A series of up-and-down bumps, suitable for jumping.

List of Choices

About the Author

Eileen Mueller lives in a cave on the side of a hill in New Zealand with four dragonets and a shape-shifter. Near her cave, there's a really cool mountain bike trail, the toughest in Wellington, called (you guessed it) Mystic Portal. Only the craziest riders go there.

Eileen writes for children and young adults. She was awarded a 2016 Sir Julius Vogel Award for Best Youth Novel with *Dragons Realm* – another *You Say Which Way* adventure.

In 2013, she won the SpecFicNZ Going Global writing contest and was first equal in NZSA NorthWrite Collaboration literary contest. Eileen co-edited *The Best of Twisty Christmas Tales* and was a sub-editor on the 2015 Sir Julius Vogel Best Collected Work, *Lost in the Museum*. A New Zealander of the Year Local Hero and marketing consultant, she managed Wellington's 2014 & 2015 Storylines children's literary festivals – having lots of fun with authors, illustrators and thousands of kids.

Eileen has free kids' books available at her website. EileenMuellerAuthor.com (Kids, please check with your parents before you download them.)

Eileen would like to thank Darian Smith for naming Hydropolis.

EILEEN MUELLER

253

Please review this book

People don't find out about good books unless we tell them. If you liked this book, please leave a review on Amazon. You'll make Eileen Mueller's day and help others to have an adventure on Mystic Portal too. Thank you.

More You Say Which Way Adventures

- Once Upon an Island
- In the Magician's House
- Pirate Island
- Volcano of Fire
- Creepy House
- Dragons Realm
- Dinosaur Canyon
- Deadline Delivery
- Between The Stars
- Island of Giants
- Lost in Lion Country
- Secrets of Glass Mountain
- Danger on Dolphin Island
- The Sorcerer's Maze Adventure Quiz